THE FOLGER LIBRARY SHAKESPEARE

Designed to make Shakespeare's classic plays available to the general reader, each edition contains a reliable text with modernized spelling and punctuation, scene-by-scene plot summaries, and explanatory notes clarifying obscure and obsolete expressions. An interpretive essay and accounts of Shakespeare's life and theater form an instructive preface to each play.

Louis B. Wright, General Editor, was the Director of the Folger Shakespeare Library from 1948 until his retirement in 1968. He is the author of *Middle-Class Culture in Elizabethan England*, *Religion and Empire*, *Shakespeare for Everyman*, and many other books and essays on the history and literature of the Tudor and Stuart periods.

Virginia Lamar, Assistant Editor, served as research assistant to the Director and Executive Secretary of the Folger Shakespeare Library from 1946 until her death in 1968. She is the author of *English Dress in the Age of Shakespeare* and *Travel and Roads in England*, and coeditor of William Strachey's *Historie of Travell into Virginia Britania*.

The Folger Shakespeare Library

The Folger Shakespeare Library in Washington, D.C., a research institute founded and endowed by Henry Clay Folger and administered by the Trustees of Amherst College, contains the world's largest collection of Shakespeareana. Although the Folger Library's primary purpose is to encourage advanced research in history and literature, it has continually exhibited a profound concern in stimulating a popular interest in the Elizabethan period.

The Folger Library General Reader's Shakespeare

THE
TWO GENTLEMEN
OF VERONA

by

WILLIAM
SHAKESPEARE

WASHINGTON SQUARE PRESS
PUBLISHED BY POCKET BOOKS

New York   London   Toronto   Sydney   Tokyo   Singapore

For orders other than by individual consumers, Washington Square Press grants a discount on the purchase of **10 or more** copies of single titles for special markets or premium use. For further details, please write to the Vice-President of Special Markets, Pocket Books, 1230 Avenue of the Americas, New York, NY 10020.

For information on how individual consumers can place orders, please write to Mail Order Department, Paramount Publishing, 200 Old Tappan Road, Old Tappan, NJ 07675.

A Washington Square Press Publication of
POCKET BOOKS, a division of Simon & Schuster Inc.
1230 Avenue of the Americas, New York, NY 10020

ISBN: 0-671-74395-3

First Pocket Books printing October 1964

14 13 12 11 10 9 8 7

WASHINGTON SQUARE PRESS and WSP colophon are registered trademarks of Simon & Schuster Inc.

Printed in the U.S.A.

Preface

This edition of *The Two Gentlemen of Verona* is designed to make available a readable text of one of Shakespeare's early comedies. In the centuries since Shakespeare, many changes have occurred in the meanings of words, and some clarification of Shakespeare's vocabulary may be helpful. To provide the reader with necessary notes in the most accessible format, we have placed them on the pages facing the text that they explain. We have tried to make these notes as brief and simple as possible. Preliminary to the text we have also included a brief statement of essential information about Shakespeare and his stage. Readers desiring more detailed information should refer to the books suggested in the references, and if still further information is needed, the bibliographies in those books will provide the necessary clues to the literature of the subject.

The early texts of Shakespeare's plays provide only scattered stage directions and no indications of setting, and it is conventional for modern editors to add these to clarify the action. Such additions, and additions to entrances and exits, as well as many indications of act and scene division, are placed in square brackets.

All illustrations are from material in the Folger Library collections.

L. B. W.
V. A. L.

December 15, 1963

Debate of Love and Friendship

The Two Gentlemen of Verona, one of Shakespeare's early plays, reveals the young dramatist dealing with a theme that excited the interest of many a Renaissance writer: the debate over the relative merits of love and friendship. Critics of the play have argued that it shows immaturity, hasty workmanship, and an unsureness of touch, because of its unrealistic ending and the utter improbabilities of the conduct of Proteus and Valentine, not to mention the meekness of Silvia, who, in the last scene, allows herself to be bandied about between the two friends without uttering a protest or a single word of comment.

To these critics, the play betrays the apprentice work of a dramatist who had not yet found his métier. This play, to be sure, lacks the finish and charm of the great comedies, but it is not so jejune as some would have us believe. Shakespeare knew what he was about and was making his contribution to a theme that others had used and would continue to use, in stage plays, in sonnet cycles, and in romantic stories. Indeed, one of the most enduring of Renaissance debates was the discussion of whether the love of woman was a sentiment more noble than the friendship that might exist between men. This friendship between men, let one hasten to say, did not connote any abnormal relationship. It was the exalted friendship that in romances led one friend to make any sacrifice required, even that of his life, for another. The literature of Greece and Rome, which influenced the Renaissance so profoundly, made frequent use of the theme of male friendship, which was emphasized by Cicero, Plutarch, and other classical authors well known to the Elizabethans.

In Shakespeare's infancy, the Master of the Children of the Chapel Royal, a certain Richard Edwards, wrote a play about the most famous of classical friendships and had his choirboys perform it at court. It was *Damon and Pythias* (ca. 1565), which was printed in 1571. After Shakespeare was already a recognized playwright in London, Henry Chettle wrote another play called *Damon and Pythias* (1600), but it has not survived. Edwards' play was concerned with the nobility of friendship between men. To the Elizabethans, the theme was also familiar from discussions in contemporary Italian writers. It appears in Castiglione's *Book of the Courtier*, translated by Sir Thomas Hoby in 1561, and in numerous other works. A frequent theme in Italian romances and plays, it was carried over into Spenser's *Faerie Queene*, Sidney's *Arcadia*, and the sonnet cycles of various English writers, including Shakespeare. In even so bourgeois a writer as Thomas Heywood, one of Shakespeare's contemporaries, the idea of the sacredness of male friendship is a convention; in *A Woman Killed with Kindness*, for example, Frankford reproaches Wendoll, not for seducing his wife, but for betraying his friendship.

Few themes are so common in Renaissance literature as this one, and Shakespeare was merely employing a literary convention in having Valentine offer Silvia to Proteus as the denouement of *The Two Gentlemen of Verona*. Readers of Elizabethan literature would have understood and accepted the convention —at least on the stage.

Yet even in this early comedy, Shakespeare goes beyond the mere conventionalities of literary tradition, conventionalities that he could have picked up from the adaptations of Italian comedies already well known in England. He gives indications of the capacity to bring stock characters to life that he was later to display in such comedies as *As You Like It* and *The Merchant of Venice*. His skill was such that characters who might have remained mere cardboard figures in a play took on the reality of human beings. The fact that Proteus, the false friend, is something more than a stage type keeps us from treating the play as one merely of convention, Sir Edmund Chambers insists. Chambers, who is not one to read much biography into the plays, does find in the characterization of Proteus some reflections from Shakespeare's *Sonnets* and the author's personal experience. "Above all," Chambers says, "one may fairly recognize in Proteus, Proteus the passionate and the perjured, not perhaps a 'portrait' of the false friend and supplanting lover, whoever he may be, of the *Sonnets*, but at least an image which would not have been drawn, or at any rate not in such deeply bitten lines, had not the friend of the *Sonnets* given Shakespeare cause to drink his portions of siren tears."

Whether Julia and Silvia are drawn from the memory of women whom the author had loved and admired is a matter for conjecture, but they have qualities of reality that make them prototypes of such later heroines as Rosalind and Viola. Thus, even early in his career, Shakespeare could not avoid giving life to characters that in the hands of a lesser dramatist would have been mere stereotypes.

The low comedy elements in *The Two Gentlemen of Verona* also foreshadow Shakespeare's use of similar situations in later plays. Launce and his dog Crab doubtless occupied a much larger place in the play than the printed text suggests, for Launce was played by the most famous clown of the Elizabethan stage, Will Kemp, and Kemp's dog was a trained beast capable of all sorts of vaudeville tricks. Shakespeare, advising the actors in the play-within-a-play in *Hamlet*, suggests that clowns sometimes ran away with a scene, and he may have had in mind Will Kemp's extempore performances: "And let those that play your clowns speak no more than is set down for them. For there be of them that will themselves laugh, to set on some quantity of barren spectators to laugh too, though in the mean time some necessary question of the play be then to be considered. That's villainous and shows a most pitiful ambition in the fool that uses it" (III, ii). Kemp had such a reputation for his comic actions that he was reputed to set an audience laughing merely by showing his grinning face. Shakespeare tried to provide adequate dialogue for Kemp, an influential member of his acting company, in order to keep him within bounds, but it is evident that he did not always manage to restrain him. The comic scenes that Shakespeare wrote for his clowns, even as they are preserved in print, reveal a humor that is still alive and viable, and humor is one of the most perishable of commodities. The scenes with Launce and his dog suggest the later appearance of Launcelot Gobbo in *The Merchant of Venice*.

But not all of the humor in *The Two Gentlemen of Verona* has an appeal for a modern audience. Speed's verbal quibbles show an Elizabethan weakness, not peculiar to Shakespeare, for wordplay that we find hard to comprehend; but this quality was also to persist. Dr. Samuel Johnson, who could not tolerate what he considered verbal nonsense, once commented:

> A quibble is to Shakespeare what luminous vapors are to the traveler; he follows it at all adventures; it is sure to lead him out of his way and sure to engulf him in the mire. It has some malignant power over his mind and its fascinations are irresistible. Whatever be the dignity or profundity of his disquisition—whether he be enlarging knowledge or exalting affection, whether he be amusing attention with incidents or enchaining it in suspense, let but a quibble spring up before him and he leaves his work unfinished. A quibble is the golden apple for which he will always turn aside from his career or stoop from his elevation. A quibble, poor and barren as it is, gave him such delight that he was content to purchase it by the sacrifice of reason, propriety, and truth. A quibble was to him the fatal Cleopatra for which he lost the world, and was content to lose it.

Although Dr. Johnson's eighteenth-century distaste strikes a responsive chord in us, Shakespeare's audiences reveled in puns and plays on words, even those as farfetched as some of Speed's, and Shakespeare never entirely gave up the verbal gymnastics that are illustrated so profusely in the early plays, *The Two Gentlemen of Verona* and *Love's Labor's Lost.*

Shakespeare chose to dramatize the story of the friendship of Proteus and Valentine because it was a subject popular in the 1590's and one likely to gain an audience. He was not one so careless of the taste of his time as to pick a tale for dramatization merely at random. A play translated, perhaps by Anthony Munday, from Luigi Pasqualigo and called *The Two Italian Gentlemen, or Fedele and Fortunio* (1585), which treated the friendship theme, had been seen on the stage long before Shakespeare's play. Some critics have thought that this comedy might have suggested the topic to Shakespeare. What his immediate source was we do not know; perhaps it was a lost play on the subject. Some of the elements in the romantic plot of Julia and Proteus are to be found in a romance written in Spanish by a Portuguese, Jorge de Montemayor, with the title *Diana enamorado,* translated by Bartholomew Young in 1582 and published in England in 1598. Since *The Two Gentlemen of Verona* was probably written sometime in 1594–95, Shakespeare could not have used the printed version, but he might have read Young's translation in manuscript. French versions of Montemayor's romance were printed at Reims in

1578 and at Paris in 1587. It is possible that Shakespeare might have read one of these.

The motif of the rope ladder with which Valentine proposed to rescue Silvia, Shakespeare could have got from Arthur Brooke's *Romeus and Juliet,* which he was reading about this time in preparation for writing *Romeo and Juliet.* Professor Oscar J. Campbell has suggested that both plot and character elements in *The Two Gentlemen of Verona* were commonplaces of numerous Italian comedies, some of which were known in England. He thinks Shakespeare could have easily picked up details for his comedy from known Italian plays. Motifs that appear in *The Two Gentlemen of Verona* are also found in stories from Boccaccio, Cinthio, and Bandello that were known to Englishmen.

Shakespeare probably put together his play from various sources, picking up bits here and there that suited his purposes. As often, he was not very careful in his allusions. For example, the reader is led to expect that the two gentlemen are to visit the Emperor's court at Milan, but as the action unfolds they are clearly at the Duke's court. At one point they appear to be still in Verona.

Dating *The Two Gentlemen of Verona* has caused difficulties. No evidence exists for fixing a precise date, but, after surveying all of the circumstances, Chambers thinks late 1594 or early 1595 suits the conditions, and this supposition, accepted by John Munro in the "London Shakespeare," has seemed reasonable to other editors.

Concerning the contemporary reception of *The Two Gentlemen of Verona* we have little evidence.

Francis Meres, in his *Palladis Tamia* of 1598, in praising Shakespeare as an equivalent of Plautus, mentions *The Two Gentlemen of Verona* among his excellent comedies. But thereafter a great silence ensues. It was included in the Folio of 1623, but until then it had not seen print.

During the Restoration and early eighteenth century the play does not appear to have been revived. Finally, in 1762, Benjamin Victor made an adaptation that increased the amount of clownery for Launce and his dog. This adaptation had a brief run at Drury Lane and then closed. Shakespeare's original story was revived at Covent Garden in 1784, and six years later another revival occurred at Drury Lane. These revivals did not create much interest. In 1821 Frederic Reynolds staged an operatic version at Covent Garden, which had a run of twenty-nine performances.

The play was revived at intervals during the nineteenth century and has had occasional performances in the twentieth century, but never with any notable success. Since the Elizabethan period the conventional treatment of the friendship theme in *The Two Gentlemen of Verona* has not been of sufficient interest to give the play an active stage life.

THE TEXT

The First Folio of 1623 was the only contemporary printing of the play. This text is reasonably free from typographical and other errors and perhaps was printed from a playhouse copy. But there are few stage directions. The present editors have accepted a few emendations proposed by earlier editors but they have adhered as closely as possible to the original of 1623.

THE AUTHOR

As early as 1598 Shakespeare was so well known as a literary and dramatic craftsman that Francis Meres, in his *Palladis Tamia: Wits Treasury*, referred in flattering terms to him as "mellifluous and honey-tongued Shakespeare," famous for his *Venus and Adonis*, his *Lucrece*, and "his sugared sonnets," which were circulating "among his private friends." Meres observes further that "as Plautus and Seneca are accounted the best for comedy and tragedy among the Latins, so Shakespeare among the English is the most excellent in both kinds for the stage," and he mentions a dozen plays that had made a name for Shakespeare. He concludes with the remark that "the Muses would speak with Shakespeare's fine filed phrase if they would speak English."

To those acquainted with the history of the Elizabethan and Jacobean periods, it is incredible that anyone should be so naïve or ignorant as to doubt the reality of Shakespeare as the author of the plays that bear his name. Yet so much nonsense has been written about other "candidates" for the plays that it is well to remind readers that no credible evidence that would stand up in a court of law has ever been adduced to prove either that Shakespeare did not write his plays or that anyone else wrote them. All the theories offered for the authorship of Francis Bacon, the Earl of Derby, the Earl of Oxford, the Earl of Hertford, Christopher Marlowe, and a score of other candidates are mere conjectures spun from the active imaginations of persons who confuse hypothesis and conjecture with evidence.

As Meres's statement of 1598 indicates, Shakespeare was already a popular playwright whose name carried weight at the box office. The obvious reputation of Shakespeare as early as 1598 makes the effort to prove him a myth one of the most absurd in the history of human perversity.

The anti-Shakespeareans talk darkly about a plot of vested interests to maintain the authorship of Shakespeare. Nobody has any vested interest in Shakespeare, but every scholar is interested in the truth and in the quality of evidence advanced by special pleaders who set forth hypotheses in place of facts.

The anti-Shakespeareans base their arguments upon a few simple premises, all of them false. These false premises are that Shakespeare was an unlettered yokel without any schooling, that nothing is known about Shakespeare, and that only a noble lord or the equivalent in background could have written the plays. The facts are that more is known about Shakespeare than about most dramatists of his day, that he had a very good education, acquired in the Stratford Grammar School, that the plays show no evidence of profound book learning, and that the knowledge of kings and courts evident in the plays is no greater than any intelligent young man could have picked up at second hand. Most anti-Shakespeareans are naïve and betray an obvious snobbery. The author of their favorite plays, they imply, must have had a college diploma framed and hung on his study wall like the one in their dentist's office, and obviously so great a writer must have had a title or some equally significant evidence of exalted social background. They forget that genius has a way of cropping up in unexpected places and that none of the great creative writers of the world got his inspiration in a college or university course.

William Shakespeare was the son of John Shakespeare of Stratford-upon-Avon, a substantial citizen of that small but busy market town in the center of the rich agricultural county of Warwick. John Shakespeare kept a shop, what we would call a general store; he dealt in wool and other produce and gradually acquired property. As a youth, John Shakespeare had learned the trade of glover and leather worker. There is no contemporary evidence that the elder Shakespeare was a butcher, though the anti-Shakespeareans like to talk about the ignorant "butcher's boy of Stratford." Their only evidence is a statement by gossipy John Aubrey, more than a century after William Shakespeare's birth, that young William followed his father's trade, and when he killed a calf, "he would do it in a high style and make a speech." We would like to believe the story true, but Aubrey is not a very credible witness.

John Shakespeare probably continued to operate a farm at Snitterfield that his father had leased. He married Mary Arden, daughter of his father's land-lord, a man of some property. The third of their eight children was William, baptized on April 26, 1564, and probably born three days before. At least, it is conventional to celebrate April 23 as his birth-day.

The Stratford records give considerable informa-tion about John Shakespeare. We know that he held several municipal offices including those of alder-man and mayor. In 1580 he was in some sort of legal difficulty and was fined for neglecting a sum-mons of the Court of Queen's Bench requiring him to appear at Westminster and be bound over to keep the peace.

As a citizen and alderman of Stratford, John Shakespeare was entitled to send his son to the grammar school free. Though the records are lost, there can be no reason to doubt that this is where young William received his education. As any stu-dent of the period knows, the grammar schools pro-vided the basic education in Latin learning and lit-erature. The Elizabethan grammar school is not to be confused with modern grammar schools. Many cultivated men of the day received all their formal education in the grammar schools. At the univer-sities in this period a student would have received little training that would have inspired him to be a creative writer. At Stratford young Shakespeare would have acquired a familiarity with Latin and some little knowledge of Greek. He would have read Latin authors and become acquainted with the plays of Plautus and Terence. Undoubtedly, in this period of his life he received that stimulation to read and explore for himself the world of ancient and modern history which he later utilized in his plays. The youngster who does not acquire this type of intellectual curiosity *before* college days rarely develops as a result of a college course the kind of mind Shakespeare demonstrated. His learning in books was anything but profound, but he clearly had the probing curiosity that sent him in search of information, and he had a keenness in the observation of nature and of humankind that finds reflection in his poetry.

There is little documentation for Shakespeare's boyhood. There is little reason why there should be. Nobody knew that he was going to be a dramatist about whom any scrap of information would be prized in the centuries to come. He was merely an active and vigorous youth of Stratford, perhaps assisting his father in his business, and no Boswell bothered to write down facts about him. The most important record that we have is a marriage license issued by the Bishop of Worcester on November 27, 1582, to permit William Shakespeare to marry Anne Hathaway, seven or eight years his senior; furthermore, the Bishop permitted the marriage after reading the banns only once instead of three times, evidence of the desire for haste. The need was explained on May 26, 1583, when the christening of Susanna, daughter of William and Anne Shakespeare, was recorded at Stratford. Two years later, on February 2, 1585, the records show the birth of twins to the Shakespeares, a boy and a girl who were christened Hamnet and Judith.

What William Shakespeare was doing in Stratford during the early years of his married life, or when he went to London, we do not know. It has been conjectured that he tried his hand at schoolteaching, but that is a mere guess. There is a legend that he left Stratford to escape a charge of poaching in the park of Sir Thomas Lucy of Charlecote, but there is no proof of this. There is also a legend that when first he came to London he earned his living by holding horses outside a playhouse and presently was given employment inside, but there is nothing better than eighteenth-century hearsay for this. How Shakespeare broke into the London theatres as a dramatist and actor we do not know. But lack of information is not surprising, for Elizabethans did not write their autobiographies, and we know even less about the lives of many writers and some men of affairs than we know about Shakespeare. By 1592 he was so well established and popular that he incurred the envy of the dramatist and pamphleteer Robert Greene, who referred to him as an "upstart crow . . . in his own conceit the only Shake-scene in a country." From this time onward, contemporary allusions and references in legal documents enable the scholar to chart Shakespeare's career with greater accuracy than is possible with most other Elizabethan dramatists.

By 1594 Shakespeare was a member of the company of actors known as the Lord Chamberlain's Men. After the accession of James I, in 1603, the company would have the sovereign for their patron and would be known as the King's Men. During the period of its greatest prosperity, this company would have as its principal theatres the Globe and the Blackfriars. Shakespeare was both an actor and a shareholder in the company. Tradition has assigned him such acting roles as Adam in *As You Like It* and the Ghost in *Hamlet*, a modest place on the stage that suggests that he may have had other duties in the management of the company. Such conclusions, however, are based on surmise.

What we do know is that his plays were popular and that he was highly successful in his vocation. His first play may have been *The Comedy of Errors*, acted perhaps in 1591. Certainly this was one of his earliest plays. The three parts of *Henry VI* were acted sometime between 1590 and 1592. Critics are not in agreement about precisely how much Shakespeare wrote of these three plays. *Richard III* probably dates from 1593. With this play Shakespeare captured the imagination of Elizabethan audiences, then enormously interested in historical plays. With *Richard III* Shakespeare also gave an interpretation pleasing to the Tudors of the rise to power of the grandfather of Queen Elizabeth. From this time onward, Shakespeare's plays followed on the stage in rapid succession: *Titus Andronicus, The Taming of the Shrew, The Two Gentlemen of Verona, Love's Labor's Lost, Romeo and Juliet, Richard II, A Midsummer Night's Dream, King John, The Merchant of Venice, Henry IV (Parts 1 and 2), Much Ado about Nothing, Henry V, Julius Cæsar, As You Like It, Twelfth Night, Hamlet, The Merry Wives of Windsor, All's Well That Ends Well, Measure for Measure, Othello, King Lear,* and nine others that followed before Shakespeare retired completely, about 1613.

In the course of his career in London, he made enough money to enable him to retire to Stratford with a competence. His purchase on May 4, 1597, of New Place, then the second-largest dwelling in Stratford, a "pretty house of brick and timber," with a handsome garden, indicates his increasing prosperity. There his wife and children lived while he busied himself in the London theatres. The summer before he acquired New Place, his life was darkened by the death of his only son, Hamnet, a child of eleven. In May, 1602, Shakespeare purchased one hundred and seven acres of fertile farmland near Stratford and a few months later bought a cottage and garden across the alley from New Place. About 1611, he seems to have returned permanently to Stratford, for the next year a legal document refers to him as "William Shakespeare of Stratford-upon-Avon . . . gentleman." To achieve the desired appellation of gentleman, William Shakespeare had seen to it that the College of Heralds in 1595 granted his father a coat of arms. In one step he thus became a second-generation gentleman.

Shakespeare's daughter Susanna made a good match in 1607 with Dr. John Hall, a prominent and prosperous Stratford physician. His second daughter, Judith, did not marry until she was thirty-two years old, and then, under somewhat scandalous circumstances, she married Thomas Quiney, a Stratford vintner. On March 25, 1616, Shakespeare made his will, bequeathing his landed property to Susanna,

£300 to Judith, certain sums to other relatives, and his second-best bed to his wife, Anne. Much has been made of the second-best bed, but the legacy probably indicates only that Anne liked that particular bed. Shakespeare, following the practice of the time, may have already arranged with Susanna for his wife's care. Finally, on April 23, 1616, the anniversary of his birth, William Shakespeare died, and he was buried on April 25 within the chancel of Trinity Church, as befitted an honored citizen. On August 6, 1623, a few months before the publication of the collected edition of Shakespeare's plays, Anne Shakespeare joined her husband in death.

THE PUBLICATION OF HIS PLAYS

During his lifetime Shakespeare made no effort to publish any of his plays, though eighteen appeared in print in single-play editions known as quartos. Some of these are corrupt versions known as "bad quartos." No quarto, so far as is known, had the author's approval. Plays were not considered "literature" any more than most radio and television scripts today are considered literature. Dramatists sold their plays outright to the theatrical companies and it was usually considered in the company's interest to keep plays from getting into print. To achieve a reputation as a man of letters, Shakespeare wrote his *Sonnets* and his narrative poems, *Venus and Adonis* and *The Rape of Lucrece*, but he probably never dreamed that his plays would establish his reputation as a literary genius. Only Ben Jonson, a man known for his colossal conceit, had the crust to call his plays *Works,* as he did when he published an edition in 1616. But men laughed at Ben Jonson.

After Shakespeare's death, two of his old colleagues in the King's Men, John Heminges and Henry Condell, decided that it would be a good thing to print, in more accurate versions than were then available, the plays already published and eighteen additional plays not previously published in quarto. In 1623 appeared *Mr. William Shakespeares Comedies, Histories, & Tragedies. Published according to the True Originall Copies. London. Printed by Isaac Iaggard and Ed. Blount.* This was the famous First Folio, a work that had the authority of Shakespeare's associates. The only play commonly attributed to Shakespeare that was omitted in the First Folio was *Pericles.* In their preface, "To the great Variety of Readers," Heminges and Condell state that whereas "you were abused with diverse stolen and surreptitious copies, maimed and deformed by the frauds and stealths of injurious impostors that exposed them, even those are now offered to your view cured and perfect of their limbs; and all the rest, absolute in their numbers, as he conceived them." What they used for printer's copy is one of the vexed problems of scholarship, and skilled bibliographers have devoted years of study to the question of the relation of the "copy" for the First Folio to Shakespeare's manuscripts. In some cases it is clear that the editors corrected printed quarto versions of the plays, probably by comparison with playhouse scripts. Whether these scripts were in Shakespeare's autograph is anybody's guess. No manuscript of any play in Shakespeare's handwriting has survived. Indeed, very few play manuscripts from this period by any author are extant. The Tudor and Stuart periods had not yet learned to prize autographs and authors' original manuscripts.

Since the First Folio contains eighteen plays not previously printed, it is the only source for these. For the other eighteen, which had appeared in quarto versions, the First Folio also has the authority of an edition prepared and overseen by Shakespeare's colleagues and professional associates. But since editorial standards in 1623 were far from strict, and Heminges and Condell were actors rather than editors by profession, the texts are sometimes careless. The printing and proofreading of the First Folio also left much to be desired, and some garbled passages have had to be corrected and emended. The "good quarto" texts have to be taken into account in preparing a modern edition.

Because of the great popularity of Shakespeare through the centuries, the First Folio has become a prized book, but it is not a very rare one, for it is estimated that 238 copies are extant. The Folger Shakespeare Library in Washington, D.C., has seventy-nine copies of the First Folio, collected by the founder, Henry Clay Folger, who believed that a collation of as many texts as possible would reveal significant facts about the text of Shakespeare's plays. Dr. Charlton Hinman, using an ingenious machine of his own invention for mechanical collating, has made many discoveries that throw light on Shakespeare's text and on printing practices of the day.

The probability is that the First Folio of 1623 had an edition of between 1,000 and 1,250 copies. It is believed that it sold for £1, which made it an expensive book, for £1 in 1623 was equivalent to something between $40 and $50 in modern purchasing power.

During the seventeenth century, Shakespeare was sufficiently popular to warrant three later editions in folio size, the Second Folio of 1632, the Third Folio of 1663–1664, and the Fourth Folio of 1685. The Third Folio added six other plays ascribed to Shakespeare, but these are apocryphal.

THE SHAKESPEAREAN THEATRE

The theatres in which Shakespeare's plays were performed were vastly different from those we know today. The stage was a platform that jutted out into the area now occupied by the first rows of seats on the main floor, what is called the "orchestra" in America and the "pit" in England. This platform had no curtain to come down at the ends of acts and scenes. And although simple stage properties were available, the Elizabethan theatre lacked both the machinery and the elaborate movable scenery of the modern theatre. In the rear of the platform stage was a curtained area that could be used as an inner room, a tomb, or any such scene that might be required. A balcony above this inner room, and perhaps balconies on the sides of the stage, could represent the upper deck of a ship, the entry to

Juliet's room, or a prison window. A trap door in the stage provided an entrance for ghosts and devils from the nether regions, and a similar trap in the canopied structure over the stage, known as the "heavens," made it possible to let down angels on a rope. These primitive stage arrangements help to account for many elements in Elizabethan plays. For example, since there was no curtain, the dramatist frequently felt the necessity of writing into his play action to clear the stage at the ends of acts and scenes. The funeral march at the end of *Hamlet* is not there merely for atmosphere; Shakespeare had to get the corpses off the stage. The lack of scenery also freed the dramatist from undue concern about the exact location of his sets, and the physical relation of his various settings to each other did not have to be worked out with the same precision as in the modern theatre.

Before London had buildings designed exclusively for theatrical entertainment, plays were given in inns and taverns. The characteristic inn of the period had an inner courtyard with rooms opening onto balconies overlooking the yard. Players could set up their temporary stages at one end of the yard and audiences could find seats on the balconies out of the weather. The poorer sort could stand or sit on the cobblestones in the yard, which was open to the sky. The first theatres followed this construction, and throughout the Elizabethan period the large public theatres had a yard in front of the stage open to the weather, with two or three tiers of covered balconies extending around the theatre. This physical structure again influenced the writing of plays. Because a dramatist wanted the actors to be heard, he frequently wrote into his play orations that could be delivered with declamatory effect. He also provided spectacle, buffoonery, and broad jests to keep the riotous groundlings in the yard entertained and quiet.

In another respect the Elizabethan theatre differed greatly from ours. It had no actresses. All women's roles were taken by boys, sometimes recruited from the boys' choirs of the London churches. Some of these youths acted their roles with great skill and the Elizabethans did not seem to be aware of any incongruity. The first actresses on the professional English stage appeared after the Restoration of Charles II, in 1660, when exiled Englishmen brought back from France practices of the French stage.

London in the Elizabethan period, as now, was the center of theatrical interest, though wandering actors from time to time traveled through the country performing in inns, halls, and the houses of the nobility. The first professional playhouse, called simply The Theatre, was erected by James Burbage, father of Shakespeare's colleague Richard Burbage, in 1576 on lands of the old Holywell Priory adjacent to Finsbury Fields, a playground and park area just north of the city walls. It had the advantage of being outside the city's jurisdiction and yet was near enough to be easily accessible. Soon after The Theatre was opened, another playhouse called The Curtain was erected in the same neighborhood. Both of these playhouses had open courtyards and were probably polygonal in shape.

About the time The Curtain opened, Richard Farrant, Master of the Children of the Chapel Royal at Windsor and of St. Paul's, conceived the idea of opening a "private" theatre in the old monastery buildings of the Blackfriars, not far from St. Paul's Cathedral in the heart of the city. This theatre was ostensibly to train the choirboys in plays for presentation at court, but Farrant managed to present plays to paying audiences and achieved considerable success until aristocratic neighbors complained and had the theatre closed. This first Blackfriars Theatre was significant, however, because it popularized the boy actors in a professional way and it paved the way for a second theatre in the Blackfriars, which Shakespeare's company took over more than thirty years later. By the last years of the sixteenth century, London had at least six professional theatres and still others were erected during the reign of James I.

The Globe Theatre, the playhouse that most people connect with Shakespeare, was erected early in 1599 on the Bankside, the area across the Thames from the city. Its construction had a dramatic beginning, for on the night of December 28, 1598, James Burbage's sons, Cuthbert and Richard, gathered together a crew who tore down the old theatre in Holywell and carted the timbers across the river to a site that they had chosen for a new playhouse. The reason for this clandestine operation was a row with the landowner over the lease to the Holywell property. The site chosen for the Globe was another playground outside of the city's jurisdiction, a region of somewhat unsavory character. Not far away was the Bear Garden, an amphitheatre devoted to the baiting of bears and bulls. This was also the region occupied by many houses of ill fame licensed by the Bishop of Winchester and the source of substantial revenue to him. But it was easily accessible either from London Bridge or by means of the cheap boats operated by the London watermen, and it had the great advantage of being beyond the authority of the Puritanical aldermen of London, who frowned on plays because they lured apprentices from work, filled their heads with improper ideas, and generally exerted a bad influence. The aldermen also complained that the crowds drawn together in the theatre helped to spread the plague.

The Globe was the handsomest theatre up to its time. It was a large building, apparently octagonal in shape, and open like its predecessors to the sky in the center, but capable of seating a large audience in its covered balconies. To erect and operate the Globe, the Burbages organized a syndicate composed of the leading members of the dramatic company, of which Shakespeare was a member. Since it was open to the weather and depended on natural light, plays had to be given in the afternoon. This caused no hardship in the long afternoons of an English summer, but in the winter the weather was a great handicap and discouraged all except the hardiest. For that reason, in 1608 Shakespeare's company was glad to take over the lease of the second Blackfriars Theatre, a substantial, roomy hall reconstructed within the framework of the old monastery building. This theatre was protected from the weather and its stage was artificially lighted by chandeliers of candles. This became the winter playhouse for Shakespeare's company and at once proved so popular that the congestion of traffic created an embarrassing problem. Stringent regulations had to be made for the movement of coaches in the vicinity. Shakespeare's company continued to use the Globe during the summer months. In 1613 a squib fired from a cannon during a performance of *Henry VIII* fell on the thatched roof and the Globe burned to the ground. The next year it was rebuilt.

London had other famous theatres. The Rose, just west of the Globe, was built by Philip Henslowe, a semiliterate denizen of the Bankside, who became one of the most important theatrical owners and producers of the Tudor and Stuart periods. What is more important for historians, he kept a detailed account book, which provides much of our information about theatrical history in his time. Another famous theatre on the Bankside was the Swan, which a Dutch priest, Johannes de Witt, visited in 1596. The crude drawing of the stage which he made was copied by his friend Arend van Buchell; it is one of the important pieces of contemporary evidence for theatrical construction. Among the other theatres, the Fortune, north of the city, on Golding Lane, and the Red Bull, even farther away from the city, off St. John's Street, were the most popular. The Red Bull, much frequented by apprentices, favored sensational and sometimes rowdy plays.

The actors who kept all of these theatres going were organized into companies under the protection of some noble patron. Traditionally actors had enjoyed a low reputation. In some of the ordinances they were classed as vagrants; in the phraseology of the time, "rogues, vagabonds, sturdy beggars, and common players" were all listed together as undesirables. To escape penalties often meted out to these characters, organized groups of actors managed to gain the protection of various personages of high degree. In the later years of Elizabeth's reign, a group flourished under the name of the Queen's Men; another group had the protection of the Lord Admiral and were known as the Lord Admiral's Men. Edward Alleyn, son-in-law of Philip Henslowe, was the leading spirit in the Lord Admiral's Men. Besides the adult companies, troupes of boy actors from time to time also enjoyed considerable popularity. Among these were the Children of Paul's and the Children of the Chapel Royal.

The company with which Shakespeare had a long association had for its first patron Henry Carey, Lord Hunsdon, the Lord Chamberlain, and hence they were known as the Lord Chamberlain's Men. After the accession of James I, they became the King's Men. This company was the great rival of the Lord Admiral's Men, managed by Henslowe and Alleyn.

All was not easy for the players in Shakespeare's time, for the aldermen of London were always eager for an excuse to close up the Blackfriars and any other theatres in their jurisdiction. The theatres outside the jurisdiction of London were not immune from interference, for they might be shut up by order of the Privy Council for meddling in politics or for various other offenses, or they might be closed in time of plague lest they spread infection. During plague times, the actors usually went on tour and played the provinces wherever they could find an audience. Particularly frightening were the plagues of 1592–1594 and 1613 when the theatres closed and the players, like many other Londoners, had to take to the country.

Though players had a low social status, they enjoyed great popularity, and one of the favorite forms of entertainment at court was the performance of plays. To be commanded to perform at court conferred great prestige upon a company of players, and printers frequently noted that fact when they published plays. Several of Shakespeare's plays were performed before the sovereign, and Shakespeare himself undoubtedly acted in some of these plays.

REFERENCES FOR FURTHER READING

Many readers will want suggestions for further reading about Shakespeare and his times. A few references will serve as guides to further study in the enormous literature on the subject. A simple and useful little book is Gerald Sanders, *A Shakespeare Primer* (New York, 1950). *A Companion to Shakespeare Studies*, edited by Harley Granville-Barker and G. B. Harrison (Cambridge, 1934), is a valuable guide. The most recent concise handbook of facts about Shakespeare is Gerald E. Bentley, *Shakespeare: A Biographical Handbook* (New Haven,

1961). More detailed but not so voluminous as to be confusing is Hazelton Spencer, *The Art and Life of William Shakespeare* (New York, 1940), which, like Sanders' and Bentley's handbooks, contains a brief, annotated list of useful books on various aspects of the subject. The most detailed and scholarly work providing complete factual information is Sir Edmund Chambers, *William Shakespeare: A Study of Facts and Problems* (2 vols., Oxford, 1930).

Among other biographies of Shakespeare, Joseph Quincy Adams, *A Life of William Shakespeare* (Boston, 1923) is still an excellent assessment of the essential facts and the traditional information, and Marchette Chute, *Shakespeare of London* (New York, 1949; paperback, 1957) stresses Shakespeare's life in the theatre. Two new biographies have recently appeared. A. L. Rowse, *William Shakespeare: A Biography* (London, 1963; New York, 1964) provides an appraisal by a distinguished English historian, who dismisses the notion that somebody else wrote Shakespeare as arrant nonsense that runs counter to known historical fact. Peter Quennell, *Shakespeare: A Biography* (Cleveland and New York, 1963) is a sensitive and intelligent survey of what is known and surmised of Shakespeare's life.

The Shakespeare Quarterly, published by the Shakespeare Association of America under the editorship of James G. McManaway, is recommended for those who wish to keep up with current Shakespearean scholarship and stage productions. The *Quarterly* includes an annual bibliography of editions and works on Shakespeare published during the previous year.

The question of the authenticity of Shakespeare's plays arouses perennial attention. The theory of hidden cryptograms in the plays is demolished by William F. and Elizebeth S. Friedman, *The Shakespearean Ciphers Examined* (New York, 1957). A succinct account of the various absurdities advanced to suggest the authorship of a multitude of candidates other than Shakespeare will be found in R. C. Churchill, *Shakespeare and His Betters* (Bloomington, Ind., 1959). Another recent discussion of the subject, *The Authorship of Shakespeare*, by James G. McManaway (Washington, D.C., 1962), presents all the evidence from contemporary records to prove the identity of Shakespeare the actor-playwright with Shakespeare of Stratford.

Scholars are not in agreement about the details of playhouse construction in the Elizabethan period. John C. Adams presents a plausible reconstruction of the Globe in *The Globe Playhouse: Its Design and Equipment* (Cambridge, Mass., 1942; 2nd rev. ed., 1961). A description with excellent drawings based on Dr. Adams' model is Irwin Smith, *Shakespeare's Globe Playhouse: A Modern Reconstruction in Text and Scale Drawings* (New York, 1956). Other sensible discussions are C. Walter Hodges, *The Globe Restored* (London, 1953) and A. M. Nagler, *Shakespeare's Stage* (New Haven, 1958). Bernard Beckerman, *Shakespeare at the Globe, 1599–1609* (New Haven, 1962; paperback, 1962) discusses Elizabethan staging and acting techniques.

A sound and readable history of the early theatres

is Joseph Quincy Adams, *Shakespearean Playhouses: A History of English Theatres from the Beginnings to the Restoration* (Boston, 1917). For detailed, factual information about the Elizabethan and seventeenth-century stages, the definitive reference works are Sir Edmund Chambers, *The Elizabethan Stage* (4 vols., Oxford, 1923) and Gerald E. Bentley, *The Jacobean and Caroline Stages* (5 vols., Oxford, 1941–1956).

Further information on the history of the theatre and related topics will be found in the following titles: T. W. Baldwin, *The Organization and Personnel of the Shakespearean Company* (Princeton, 1927); Lily Bess Campbell, *Scenes and Machines on the English Stage during the Renaissance* (Cambridge, 1923); Esther Cloudman Dunn, *Shakespeare in America* (New York, 1939); George C. D. Odell, *Shakespeare from Betterton to Irving* (2 vols., London, 1931); Arthur Colby Sprague, *Shakespeare and the Actors: The Stage Business in His Plays (1660–1905)* (Cambridge, Mass., 1944) and *Shakespearian Players and Performances* (Cambridge, Mass., 1953); Leslie Hotson, *The Commonwealth and Restoration Stage* (Cambridge, Mass., 1928); Alwin Thaler, *Shakspere to Sheridan: A Book about the Theatre of Yesterday and To-day* (Cambridge, Mass., 1922); George C. Branam, *Eighteenth-Century Adaptations of Shakespeare's Tragedies* (Berkeley, 1956); C. Beecher Hogan, *Shakespeare in the Theatre, 1701–1800* (Oxford, 1957); Ernest Bradlee Watson, *Sheridan to Robertson: A Study of the 19th-Century London Stage* (Cambridge, Mass., 1926);

and Enid Welsford, *The Court Masque* (Cambridge, Mass., 1927).

A brief account of the growth of Shakespeare's reputation is F. E. Halliday, *The Cult of Shakespeare* (London, 1947). A more detailed discussion is given in Augustus Ralli, *A History of Shakespearian Criticism* (2 vols., Oxford, 1932; New York, 1958). Harley Granville-Barker, *Prefaces to Shakespeare* (5 vols., London, 1927–1948; 2 vols., London, 1958) provides stimulating critical discussion of the plays. An older classic of criticism is Andrew C. Bradley, *Shakespearean Tragedy: Lectures on Hamlet, Othello, King Lear, Macbeth* (London, 1904; paperback, 1955). Sir Edmund Chambers, *Shakespeare: A Survey* (London, 1935; paperback, 1958) contains short, sensible essays on thirty-four of the plays, originally written as introductions to single-play editions.

For the history plays see Lily Bess Campbell, *Shakespeare's "Histories": Mirrors of Elizabethan Policy* (Cambridge, 1947); John Palmer, *Political Characters of Shakespeare* (London, 1945; 1961); E. M. W. Tillyard, *Shakespeare's History Plays* (London, 1948); Irving Ribner, *The English History Play in the Age of Shakespeare* (Princeton, 1947); and Max M. Reese, *The Cease of Majesty* (London, 1961).

The comedies are illuminated by the following studies: C. L. Barber, *Shakespeare's Festive Comedy: A Study of Dramatic Form and Its Relation to Social Custom* (Princeton, 1959); John Russell Brown, *Shakespeare and His Comedies* (London, 1957); H. B. Charlton, *Shakespearian Comedy*

(London, 1938; 4th ed., 1949); W. W. Lawrence, *Shakespeare's Problem Comedies* (New York, 1931); and Thomas M. Parrott, *Shakespearean Comedy* (New York, 1949).

Further discussions of Shakespeare's tragedies, in addition to Bradley, already cited, are contained in H. B. Charlton, *Shakespearian Tragedy* (Cambridge, 1948); Willard Farnham, *The Medieval Heritage of Elizabethan Tragedy* (Berkeley, 1936) and *Shakespeare's Tragic Frontier: The World of His Final Tragedies* (Berkeley, 1950); and Harold S. Wilson, *On the Design of Shakespearian Tragedy* (Toronto, 1957).

The "Roman" plays are treated in M. M. MacCallum, *Shakespeare's Roman Plays and Their Background* (London, 1910) and J. C. Maxwell, "Shakespeare's Roman Plays, 1900–1956," *Shakespeare Survey 10* (Cambridge, 1957), 1-11.

Kenneth Muir, *Shakespeare's Sources: Comedies and Tragedies* (London, 1957) discusses Shakespeare's use of source material. The sources themselves have been reprinted several times. Among old editions are John P. Collier (ed.), *Shakespeare's Library* (2 vols., London, 1850), Israel C. Gollancz (ed.), *The Shakespeare Classics* (12 vols., London, 1907–26), and W. C. Hazlitt (ed.), *Shakespeare's Library* (6 vols., London, 1875). A modern edition is being prepared by Geoffrey Bullough with the title *Narrative and Dramatic Sources of Shakespeare* (London and New York, 1957–). Four volumes, covering the sources for the comedies and histories, have been published to date.

In addition to the second edition of *Webster's*

New International Dictionary, which contains most of the unusual words used by Shakespeare, the following reference works are helpful: Edwin A. Abbott, *A Shakespearian Grammar* (London, 1872); C. T. Onions, *A Shakespeare Glossary* (2nd rev. ed., Oxford, 1925); and Eric Partridge, *Shakepeare's Bawdy* (New York, 1948; paperback, 1960).

Some knowledge of the social background of the period in which Shakespeare lived is important for a full understanding of his work. A brief, clear, and accurate account of Tudor history is S. T. Bindoff, *The Tudors,* in the Penguin series. A readable general history is G. M. Trevelyan, *The History of England,* first published in 1926 and available in numerous editions. The same author's *English Social History,* first published in 1942 and also available in many editions, provides fascinating information about England in all periods. Sir John Neale, *Queen Elizabeth* (London, 1935; paperback, 1957) is the best study of the great Queen. Various aspects of life in the Elizabethan period are treated in Louis B. Wright, *Middle-Class Culture in Elizabethan England* (Chapel Hill, N.C., 1935; reprinted Ithaca, N.Y., 1958). *Shakespeare's England: An Account of the Life and Manners of His Age,* edited by Sidney Lee and C. T. Onions (2 vols., Oxford, 1917), provides a large amount of information on many aspects of Elizabethan life. A fascinating survey of the period will be found in Muriel St. C. Byrne, *Elizabethan Life in Town and Country* (London, 1925; rev. ed., 1954; paperback, 1961).

The Folger Library is issuing a series of illustrated booklets entitled "Folger Booklets on Tudor and

Stuart Civilization," printed and distributed by
Cornell University Press. Published to date are the
following titles:

D. W. Davies, *Dutch Influences on English Culture, 1558–1625*

Giles E. Dawson, *The Life of William Shakespeare*

Ellen C. Eyler, *Early English Gardens and Garden
Books*

John R. Hale, *The Art of War and Renaissance
England*

Virginia A. LaMar, *English Dress in the Age of
Shakespeare*

———, *Travel and Roads in England*

John L. Lievsay, *The Elizabethan Image of Italy*

James G. McManaway, *The Authorship of Shakespeare*

Dorothy E. Mason, *Music in Elizabethan England*

Garrett Mattingly, *The "Invincible" Armada and
Elizabethan England*

Boies Penrose, *Tudor and Early Stuart Voyaging*

Conyers Read, *The Government of England under
Elizabeth*

Albert J. Schmidt, *The Yeoman in Tudor and
Stuart England*

Lilly C. Stone, *English Sports and Recreations*

Craig R. Thompson, *The Bible in English, 1525–
1611*

———, *The English Church in the Sixteenth Century*

———, *Schools in Tudor England*

———, *Universities in Tudor England*

Louis B. Wright, *Shakespeare's Theatre and the Dramatic Tradition*

At intervals the Folger Library plans to gather these booklets in hard-bound volumes. The first is *Life and Letters in Tudor and Stuart England, First Folger Series,* edited by Louis B. Wright and Virginia A. LaMar (published for the Folger Shakespeare Library by Cornell University Press, 1962). The volume contains eleven of the separate booklets.

The Names of All the Actors

Duke [of Milan], father to *Silvia*.

Valentine,
Proteus, } the two gentlemen.

Antonio, father to *Proteus*.

Thurio, a foolish rival to *Valentine*.

Eglamour, agent for *Silvia* in her escape.

Host where *Julia* lodges.

Outlaws with *Valentine*.

Speed, a clownish servant to *Valentine*.

Launce, the like to *Proteus*.

Panthino, servant to *Antonio*.

Julia, beloved of *Proteus*.

Silvia, beloved of *Valentine*.

Lucetta, waiting woman to *Julia*.

[Servants, Musicians.

SCENE: *Verona; Milan; and a forest on the frontiers of Mantua.*]

THE
TWO GENTLEMEN
OF
VERONA

ACT I

I.i. Valentine, about to leave Verona to see something of the world, says good-by to his friend Proteus. Speed, the servant of Proteus, reports the reception of a letter that his master has sent to Julia, with whom Proteus is in love. Her reaction was not encouraging and Proteus resolves to send a more impressive messenger the next time.

---

8. **shapeless:** aimless.

10. **would:** would wish.

12. **haply:** perhaps.

17. **grievance:** distress.

18. **beadsman:** one who prays for another's salvation. Beadsmen were often needy persons who prayed for their patrons in return for food and maintenance.

Leander crossing the Hellespont. From Musaeus, *Opusculum de Herone et Leandro* (1538).

ACT I

Scene I. [Verona. An open place.]

[*Enter*] *Valentine and Proteus.*

Val. Cease to persuade, my loving Proteus:
Homekeeping youth have ever homely wits.
Were't not affection chains thy tender days
To the sweet glances of thy honored love,
I rather would entreat thy company   5
To see the wonders of the world abroad
Than, living dully sluggardized at home,
Wear out thy youth with shapeless idleness.
But since thou lovest, love still, and thrive therein,
Even as I would, when I to love begin.   10
   Pro. Wilt thou be gone? Sweet Valentine, adieu!
Think on thy Proteus when thou, haply, seest
Some rare noteworthy object in thy travel.
Wish me partaker in thy happiness
When thou dost meet good hap; and in thy danger, 15
If ever danger do environ thee,
Commend thy grievance to my holy prayers,
For I will be thy beadsman, Valentine.
   Val. And on a love book pray for my success?
   Pro. Upon some book I love I'll pray for thee.   20
   Val. That's on some shallow story of deep love:

1

22. **Leander:** the lover of Hero, for whom he swam the Hellespont nightly until he was drowned in a storm.

27. **give me not the boots:** don't torment me. The phrase possibly derives from the torture instrument known as the "boot."

28. **boots:** avails.

34. **watchful:** wakeful.

35. **haply:** perhaps; **hapless:** unlucky.

37. **However:** in any case.

39. **by your circumstance:** in a roundabout manner.

40. **circumstance:** the **circumstance** in which he ultimately finds himself as a lover.

46. **canker:** cankerworm.

52. **prime:** spring.

The torture known as the boot. From Jean Milles de Souvigny, *Praxis criminis persequendi* (1541).

How young Leander crossed the Hellespont.
  Pro. That's a deep story of a deeper love;
For he was more than over shoes in love.
  Val. 'Tis true; for you are over boots in love,   25
And yet you never swum the Hellespont.
  Pro. Over the boots? Nay, give me not the boots.
  Val. No, I will not, for it boots thee not.
  Pro.   What?
  Val. To be in love, where scorn is bought with   30
     groans,
Coy looks with heartsore sighs, one fading moment's
     mirth
With twenty watchful, weary, tedious nights:
If haply won, perhaps a hapless gain;   35
If lost, why then a grievous labor won;
However, but a folly bought with wit,
Or else a wit by folly vanquished.
  Pro. So, by your circumstance, you call me fool.
  Val. So, by your circumstance, I fear you'll prove.   40
  Pro. 'Tis love you cavil at; I am not Love.
  Val. Love is your master, for he masters you;
And he that is so yoked by a fool,
Methinks should not be chronicled for wise.
  Pro. Yet writers say, as in the sweetest bud   45
The eating canker dwells, so eating love
Inhabits in the finest wits of all.
  Val. And writers say, as the most forward bud
Is eaten by the canker ere it blow,
Even so by love the young and tender wit   50
Is turned to folly, blasting in the bud,
Losing his verdure even in the prime,

55. **fond:** foolish.

56. **road:** harbor where the ship is anchored.

58. **bring:** escort.

62. **Betideth:** occurs.

63. **visit:** comfort.

72. **thought:** melancholy.

73. **save you:** God save you (a conventional greeting).

74. **parted:** departed.

76. **sheep:** Speed takes advantage of the fact that **shipped** and **sheep** were interchangeably pronounced to make a pun on the two words.

78. **And if:** if.

And all the fair effects of future hopes.
But wherefore waste I time to counsel thee
That art a votary to fond desire?   55
Once more adieu! My father at the road
Expects my coming, there to see me shipped.
   Pro. And thither will I bring thee, Valentine.
   Val. Sweet Proteus, no: now let us take our leave.
To Milan let me hear from thee by letters   60
Of thy success in love and what news else
Betideth here in absence of thy friend;
And I likewise will visit thee with mine.
   Pro. All happiness bechance to thee in Milan!
   Val. As much to you at home! and so, farewell.   65
                                      Exit.

   Pro. He after honor hunts, I after love:
He leaves his friends to dignify them more;
I leave myself, my friends, and all, for love.
Thou, Julia, thou hast metamorphosed me,
Made me neglect my studies, lose my time,   70
War with good counsel, set the world at nought;
Made wit with musing weak, heart sick with thought.

[*Enter Speed.*]

   Speed. Sir Proteus, save you! Saw you my master?
   Pro. But now he parted hence to embark for Milan.
   Speed. Twenty to one, then, he is shipped already,   75
And I have played the sheep in losing him.
   Pro. Indeed, a sheep doth very often stray,
And if the shepherd be awhile away.

82. **my horns are his horns:** a typical reference to the proverbial horns of the man whose wife has been unfaithful. In a more general sense, Speed says that his disgrace is also his master's.

87. **circumstance:** detailed argument.

88. **It shall go hard but I'll prove it:** i.e., it will be hard to prevent me from proving it.

96. **baa:** a pun on the sheep's cry and a "bah" of disgust.

100. **laced mutton:** usually applied to a loose woman or prostitute, perhaps from a more general meaning of a woman who allures men.

104. **overcharged:** overcrowded.

105. **stick:** slaughter, with a ribald double meaning.

106. **pound:** (1) impound (pen up); (2) pummel.

108. **a pound:** a tip of a pound in money.

Speed. You conclude that my master is a shepherd,
  then, and I a sheep?   80

Pro. I do.

Speed. Why then, my horns are his horns, whether
  I wake or sleep.

Pro. A silly answer and fitting well a sheep.

Speed. This proves me still a sheep.   85

Pro. True; and thy master a shepherd.

Speed. Nay, that I can deny by a circumstance.

Pro. It shall go hard but I'll prove it by another.

Speed. The shepherd seeks the sheep, and not the
sheep the shepherd; but I seek my master, and my   90
master seeks not me: therefore I am no sheep.

Pro. The sheep for fodder follow the shepherd; the
shepherd for food follows not the sheep: thou for
wages followest thy master; thy master for wages follows not thee: therefore thou art a sheep.   95

Speed. Such another proof will make me cry "baa."

Pro. But, dost thou hear? Gavest thou my letter to
Julia?

Speed. Ay, sir: I, a lost mutton, gave your letter to
her, a laced mutton, and she, a laced mutton, gave   100
me, a lost mutton, nothing for my labor.

Pro. Here's too small a pasture for such store of
muttons.

Speed. If the ground be overcharged, you were best
stick her.   105

Pro. Nay, in that you are astray: 'twere best pound
you.

Speed. Nay, sir, less than a pound shall serve me
for carrying your letter.

117. **noddy:** fool.

124. **fain to bear with:** forced to be patient with.

129. **Beshrew me:** the Devil take me (a casual oath).

131. **open:** reveal.

Pro. You mistake; I mean the pound, a pinfold.   110

Speed. From a pound to a pin? Fold it over and over,

'Tis threefold too little for carrying a letter to your lover.

Pro. But what said she?   115

Speed. [*First nodding*] Ay.

Pro. Nod—Ay; why, that's noddy.

Speed. You mistook, sir: I say, she did nod;
And you ask me if she did nod, and I say, "Ay."

Pro. And that set together is noddy.   120

Speed. Now you have taken the pains to set it together, take it for your pains.

Pro. No, no; you shall have it for bearing the letter.

Speed. Well, I perceive I must be fain to bear with you.   125

Pro. Why, sir, how do you bear with me?

Speed. Marry, sir, the letter, very orderly,
Having nothing but the word "noddy" for my pains.

Pro. Beshrew me, but you have a quick wit.

Speed. And yet it cannot overtake your slow purse.   130

Pro. Come, come, open the matter in brief: what said she?

Speed. Open your purse, that the money and the matter may be both at once delivered.

Pro. Well, sir, here is for your pains. What said   135
she?

Speed. Truly, sir, I think you'll hardly win her.

Pro. Why, couldst thou perceive so much from her?

Speed. Sir, I could perceive nothing at all from her;
no, not so much as a ducat for delivering your letter: 140

148. **testerned me:** given me a testern (a small coin).

149. **commend you:** give your greetings.

153. **destined to a drier death:** i.e., hanging. Cf. the proverb "He that is born to be hanged shall never be drowned."

155. **deign:** condescend to accept.

156. **post:** messenger.

<hr/>

I.ii. Julia discusses with her maid, Lucetta, the comparative merits of her many suitors. Lucetta advises that of them all Proteus loves her best and gives her a letter that has come by the hand of Valentine's page. Julia pretends anger that Lucetta should act as a go-between but finally reads the letter and is moved by its contents.

<hr/>

5. **encounter:** solicit.

7. **Please you:** if you please to.

and being so hard to me that brought your mind, I
fear she'll prove as hard to you in telling your mind.
Give to her no token but stones, for she's as hard as
steel.

Pro. What said she? nothing?   145

Speed. No, not so much as "Take this for thy
pains." To testify your bounty, I thank you, you have
testerned me; in requital whereof, henceforth carry
your letters yourself. And so, sir, I'll commend you
to my master.   150

Pro. Go, go, be gone, to save your ship from wrack,
Which cannot perish, having thee aboard,
Being destined to a drier death on shore.   *Exit Speed.*
I must go send some better messenger:
I fear my Julia would not deign my lines,   155
Receiving them from such a worthless post.

                        Exit.

Scene II. [Verona. Garden of Julia's house.]

Enter Julia and Lucetta.

Jul. But say, Lucetta, now we are alone,
Wouldst thou, then, counsel me to fall in love?

Luc. Ay, madam, so you stumble not unheedfully.

Jul. Of all the fair resort of gentlemen
That every day with parle encounter me,   5
In thy opinion which is worthiest love?

Luc. Please you repeat their names, I'll show my
    mind

17. **passion:** outburst.
19. **passing:** surpassing.
21. **censure:** sit in judgment.
30. **moved:** courted.

DONZELLA
NOBILE
ORNATA.

Costume of a woman of Mantua. From Cesare Vecellio, *Habiti antichi et moderni* (1590).

According to my shallow, simple skill.

   Jul. What thinkst thou of the fair Sir Eglamour?   10

   Luc. As of a knight well-spoken, neat, and fine;

But, were I you, he never should be mine.

   Jul. What thinkst thou of the rich Mercatio?

   Luc. Well of his wealth; but of himself, so-so.

   Jul. What thinkst thou of the gentle Proteus?   15

   Luc. Lord, Lord! to see what folly reigns in us!

   Jul. How now! what means this passion at his
     name?

   Luc. Pardon, dear madam: 'tis a passing shame

That I, unworthy body as I am,   20

Should censure thus on lovely gentlemen.

   Jul. Why not on Proteus, as of all the rest?

   Luc. Then thus: of many good I think him best.

   Jul. Your reason?

   Luc. I have no other but a woman's reason: 25

I think him so because I think him so.

   Jul. And wouldst thou have me cast my love on
     him?

   Luc. Ay, if you thought your love not cast away.

   Jul. Why, he, of all the rest, hath never moved me.   30

   Luc. Yet he, of all the rest, I think, best loves ye.

   Jul. His little speaking shows his love but small.

   Luc. Fire that's closest kept burns most of all.

   Jul. They do not love that do not show their love.

   Luc. O, they love least that let men know their   35
     love.

   Jul. I would I knew his mind.

   Luc. Peruse this paper, madam.

   Jul. "To Julia." Say, from whom?

44. **in the way:** available.
46. **broker:** go-between.
53. **fee:** reward.
56. **o'erlooked:** read.
58. **pray her to a fault:** i.e., ask her to give me the letter.
68. **angerly:** angrily.

Luc. That the contents will show.   40
Jul. Say, say, who gave it thee?
Luc. Sir Valentine's page; and sent, I think, from
    Proteus.
He would have given it you; but I, being in the way,
Did in your name receive it. Pardon the fault, I pray.   45
    Jul. Now, by my modesty, a goodly broker!
Dare you presume to harbor wanton lines?
To whisper and conspire against my youth?
Now, trust me, 'tis an office of great worth,
And you an officer fit for the place.   50
There, take the paper; see it be returned;
Or else return no more into my sight.
    Luc. To plead for love deserves more fee than hate.
    Jul. Will ye be gone?
    Luc.   That you may ruminate. *Exit.* 55
    Jul. And yet I would I had o'erlooked the letter.
It were a shame to call her back again
And pray her to a fault for which I chid her.
What fool is she, that knows I am a maid
And would not force the letter to my view!   60
Since maids, in modesty, say "no" to that
Which they would have the profferer construe "ay."
Fie, fie, how wayward is this foolish love,
That like a testy babe will scratch the nurse
And presently, all humbled, kiss the rod!   65
How churlishly I chid Lucetta hence,
When willingly I would have had her here!
How angerly I taught my brow to frown,
When inward joy enforced my heart to smile!
My penance is to call Lucetta back   70

76. **stomach:** the word meant "anger," as well as "appetite."

90. **toys:** trifles.

92. **heavy:** (1) serious; (2) weighty; **light:** wanton.

93. **Belike:** perhaps; **burden:** (1) refrain; (2) weight.

97. **minion:** creature.

And ask remission for my folly past.
What, ho! Lucetta!

[Enter Lucetta.]

Luc.   What would your Ladyship?
Jul. Is't near dinnertime?
Luc.   I would it were;   75
That you might kill your stomach on your meat
And not upon your maid.
   Jul. What is't that you took up so gingerly?
   Luc. Nothing.
   Jul. Why didst thou stoop, then?   80
   Luc. To take a paper up that I let fall.
   Jul. And is that paper nothing?
   Luc. Nothing concerning me.
   Jul. Then let it lie for those that it concerns.
   Luc. Madam, it will not lie where it concerns,   85
Unless it have a false interpreter.
   Jul. Some love of yours hath writ to you in rhyme.
   Luc. That I might sing it, madam, to a tune.
Give me a note: your Ladyship can set.
   Jul. As little by such toys as may be possible.   90
Best sing it to the tune of "Light o' Love."
   Luc. It is too heavy for so light a tune.
   Jul. Heavy! Belike it hath some burden, then?
   Luc. Ay, and melodious were it, would you sing it.
   Jul. And why not you?   95
   Luc.   I cannot reach so high.
   Jul. Let's see your song. How now, minion!
   Luc. Keep tune there still, so you will sing it out:

105. **mean:** voice in the middle range.

107. **bid the base for:** act on behalf of (a phrase from the game "Prisoner's Base").

109. **coil:** to-do.

112. **makes it strange:** pretends that the letter is displeasing.

119. **several:** separate.

126. **throughly:** thoroughly.

127. **sovereign:** healing.

And yet methinks I do not like this tune.

  Jul. You do not?   100

  Luc.   No, madam, 'tis too sharp.

  Jul. You, minion, are too saucy.

  Luc. Nay, now you are too flat,

And mar the concord with too harsh a descant:

There wanteth but a mean to fill your song.   105

  Jul. The mean is drowned with your unruly bass.

  Luc. Indeed, I bid the base for Proteus.

  Jul. This babble shall not henceforth trouble me.

Here is a coil with protestation!   *[Tears the letter.]*

Go get you gone, and let the papers lie: 110

You would be fingering them to anger me.

  Luc. She makes it strange, but she would be best

    pleased

To be so angered with another letter.   *[Exit.]*

  Jul. Nay, would I were so angered with the same! 115

O hateful hands, to tear such loving words!

Injurious wasps, to feed on such sweet honey

And kill the bees, that yield it, with your stings!

I'll kiss each several paper for amends.

Look, here is writ "kind Julia." Unkind Julia!   120

As in revenge of thy ingratitude,

I throw thy name against the bruising stones,

Trampling contemptuously on thy disdain.

And here is writ "love-wounded Proteus."

Poor wounded name! My bosom, as a bed,   125

Shall lodge thee till thy wound be throughly healed;

And thus I search it with a sovereign kiss.

But twice or thrice was "Proteus" written down.

Be calm, good wind, blow not a word away,

135. **passionate:** grief-stricken.
137. **sith:** since.
142. **stays:** waits.
145. **respect:** are concerned about.
146. **taken up:** rebuked.
147. **for:** for fear of.
148. **a month's mind to:** i.e., a yearning for; they attract her strongly.
150. **wink:** close my eyes.

Till I have found each letter in the letter,   130
Except mine own name: that some whirlwind bear
Unto a ragged, fearful-hanging rock
And throw it thence into the raging sea!
Lo, here in one line is his name twice writ,
"Poor forlorn Proteus, passionate Proteus,   135
To the sweet Julia": that I'll tear away.
And yet I will not, sith so prettily
He couples it to his complaining names.
Thus will I fold them one upon another:
Now kiss, embrace, contend, do what you will.   140

[Re-enter Lucetta.]

Luc. Madam,
Dinner is ready, and your father stays.
Jul. Well, let us go.
Luc. What, shall these papers lie like telltales here?
Jul. If you respect them, best to take them up.   145
Luc. Nay, I was taken up for laying them down:
Yet here they shall not lie, for catching cold.
Jul. I see you have a month's mind to them.
Luc. Ay, madam, you may say what sights you see;
I see things too, although you judge I wink.   150
Jul. Come, come, will't please you go?

Exeunt.

I.iii. Proteus' father Antonio is advised by Panthino that his son will lack something in polish if he stays at home and sees nothing of the world. This advice coinciding with his own thinking, Antonio decides to send Proteus after Valentine to the Emperor's court. In the meantime, Proteus has had a letter from Julia declaring her love. He protests in vain his father's order for departure and is forced to resign himself to parting from his love.

━━━━━━━━━━━━━━━━━━

1. **sad:** grave.

10. **discover:** explore.

13. **meet:** fitted.

16. **impeachment to his age:** i.e., grounds for doubting his wisdom when he grows old.

19. **hammering:** pondering continuously.

21. **perfect:** fully accomplished (not **perfect** in a moral sense).

Scene III. [Verona. Antonio's house.]

Enter Antonio and Panthino.

Ant. Tell me, Panthino, what sad talk was that
Wherewith my brother held you in the cloister?
   Pan. 'Twas of his nephew Proteus, your son.
   Ant. Why, what of him?
   Pan.   He wondered that your Lordship   5
Would suffer him to spend his youth at home,
While other men, of slender reputation,
Put forth their sons to seek preferment out;
Some to the wars, to try their fortune there;
Some to discover islands far away;   10
Some to the studious universities.
For any, or for all these exercises,
He said that Proteus your son was meet
And did request me to importune you
To let him spend his time no more at home,   15
Which would be great impeachment to his age,
In having known no travel in his youth.
   Ant. Nor needst thou much importune me to that
Whereon this month I have been hammering.
I have considered well his loss of time,   20
And how he cannot be a perfect man,
Not being tried and tutored in the world.
Experience is by industry achieved
And perfected by the swift course of time.
Then, tell me, whither were I best to send him?   25

28. **Emperor:** Shakespeare is careless in his references and never makes the distinction clear between the court of the Duke of Milan and the court of the Emperor of the Holy Roman Empire. The Emperor Charles V for a time held suzerainty over Milan.

34. **be in eye of:** be a witness to.

44. **commend:** offer.

46. **in good time:** "most opportune" (as he sees Proteus approaching); **break with:** inform.

CAVALLO LEGGIERO:

A knight tilting. From Cesare Vecellio, *Habiti antichi et moderni* (1590).

13

Pan. I think your Lordship is not ignorant
How his companion, youthful Valentine,
Attends the Emperor in his royal court.

   Ant. I know it well.

   Pan. 'Twere good, I think, your Lordship sent him   30
    thither:
There shall he practice tilts and tournaments,
Hear sweet discourse, converse with noblemen,
And be in eye of every exercise
Worthy his youth and nobleness of birth.   35

   Ant. I like thy counsel; well hast thou advised:
And that thou mayst perceive how well I like it,
The execution of it shall make known.
Even with the speediest expedition
I will dispatch him to the Emperor's court.   40

   Pan. Tomorrow, may it please you, Don Alphonso,
With other gentlemen of good esteem,
Are journeying to salute the Emperor
And to commend their service to his will.

   Ant. Good company: with them shall Proteus go: 45
And in good time! Now will we break with him.

[*Enter Proteus.*]

   Pro. Sweet love! sweet lines! sweet life!
Here is her hand, the agent of her heart;
Here is her oath for love, her honor's pawn.
O, that our fathers would applaud our loves,   50
To seal our happiness with their consents!
O heavenly Julia!

   Ant. How now! What letter are you reading there?

55. **commendations:** greetings.

60. **graced:** honored or favored.

62. **how stand you affected to his wish:** how does his wish appeal to you.

65. **something sorted:** somewhat in accord.

71. **exhibition:** allowance.

76. **Look what:** whatever.

IMPERA- TORE.

The Emperor of the Holy Roman Empire. From Cesare Vecellio, *Habiti antichi et moderni* (1590).

Pro. May't please your Lordship, 'tis a word or two
Of commendations sent from Valentine,   55
Delivered by a friend that came from him.
    Ant. Lend me the letter: let me see what news.
    Pro. There is no news, my lord, but that he writes
How happily he lives, how well beloved
And daily graced by the Emperor,   60
Wishing me with him, partner of his fortune.
    Ant. And how stand you affected to his wish?
    Pro. As one relying on your Lordship's will
And not depending on his friendly wish.
    Ant. My will is something sorted with his wish.   65
Muse not that I thus suddenly proceed;
For what I will, I will, and there an end.
I am resolved that thou shalt spend some time
With Valentinus in the Emperor's court.
What maintenance he from his friends receives,   70
Like exhibition thou shalt have from me.
Tomorrow be in readiness to go.
Excuse it not, for I am peremptory.
    Pro. My lord, I cannot be so soon provided:
Please you, deliberate a day or two.   75
    Ant. Look what thou wantst shall be sent after
        thee:
No more of stay! tomorrow thou must go.
Come on, Panthino: you shall be employed
To hasten on his expedition.   80
                    Exeunt Antonio and Panthino.
    Pro. Thus have I shunned the fire for fear of burn-
        ing
And drenched me in the sea, where I am drowned.

85. **take exceptions:** find reasons to object.
86. **vantage:** opportunity; **mine own excuse:** i.e., the pretense that the letter came from Valentine.
87. **excepted:** i.e., ruled her out.
88. **spring:** early beginning.

I feared to show my father Julia's letter,
Lest he should take exceptions to my love;   85
And with the vantage of mine own excuse
Hath he excepted most against my love.
O, how this spring of love resembleth
The uncertain glory of an April day,
Which now shows all the beauty of the sun,   90
And by and by a cloud takes all away!

[*Enter Panthino.*]

Pan. Sir Proteus, your father calls for you:
He is in haste; therefore, I pray you, go.
Pro. Why, this it is: my heart accords thereto,
And yet a thousand times it answers "no."   95

Exeunt.

THE
TWO GENTLEMEN
OF
VERONA

ACT II

II.i. Valentine has fallen passionately in love with Silvia, daughter of the Duke of Milan. Although she has not yet committed herself directly, she has commissioned him to write a love letter for her, ostensibly to another lover, but she leaves the letter with Valentine. Speed points out to his master that Silvia is declaring her own love in this roundabout manner and that the letter is meant for him.

▬▬▬▬▬▬▬▬▬▬▬

4. **one: one** and **on** were not always distinguished in pronunciation. There are many contemporary puns on the two words.

21. **wreathe your arms:** fold your arms (in an attitude of pensive melancholy).

ACT II

Scene I. [Milan. The Duke's palace.]

Enter Valentine and Speed.

Speed. Sir, your glove.

Val.   Not mine: my gloves are on.

Speed. Why, then, this may be yours, for this is but
one.

Val. Ha! let me see: ay, give it me, it's mine.   5
Sweet ornament that decks a thing divine!
Ah, Silvia, Silvia!

Speed. Madam Silvia! Madam Silvia!

Val. How now, sirrah?

Speed. She is not within hearing, sir.   10

Val. Why, sir, who bade you call her?

Speed. Your Worship, sir, or else I mistook.

Val. Well, you'll still be too forward.

Speed. And yet I was last chidden for being too
slow.   15

Val. Go to, sir. Tell me, do you know Madam
Silvia?

Speed. She that your Worship loves?

Val. Why, how know you that I am in love?

Speed. Marry, by these special marks: first, you   20
have learned, like Sir Proteus, to wreathe your arms

16

28. **Hallowmas:** All Saints' Day.
31. **presently:** immediately; **sadly:** seriously.
33. **that:** so that.
51. **hard-favored:** unattractive.
52. **well-favored:** graciously disposed.

like a malcontent; to relish a love song, like a robin
redbreast; to walk alone, like one that had the pes-
tilence; to sigh, like a schoolboy that had lost his
ABC; to weep, like a young wench that had buried   25
her grandam; to fast, like one that takes diet; to
watch, like one that fears robbing; to speak puling,
like a beggar at Hallowmas. You were wont, when
you laughed, to crow like a cock; when you walked,
to walk like one of the lions. When you fasted, it was   30
presently after dinner; when you looked sadly, it was
for want of money: and now you are metamorphosed
with a mistress that, when I look on you, I can hardly
think you my master.

Val. Are all these things perceived in me?   35

Speed. They are all perceived without ye.

Val. Without me? They cannot.

Speed. Without you? Nay, that's certain, for, without you were so simple, none else would: but you
are so without these follies, that these follies are   40
within you and shine through you like the water in
an urinal, that not an eye that sees you but is a physician to comment on your malady.

Val. But tell me, dost thou know My Lady Silvia?

Speed. She that you gaze on so as she sits at sup-   45
per?

Val. Hast thou observed that? Even she, I mean.

Speed. Why, sir, I know her not.

Val. Dost thou know her by my gazing on her and
yet knowst her not?   50

Speed. Is she not hard-favored, sir?

Val. Not so fair, boy, as well-favored.

58. favor: grace.

63. counts of her beauty: i.e., credits her with beauty.

66. since she was deformed: Speed means that when Valentine fell in love, his emotion transfigured his mistress so that he no longer sees her true appearance.

Speed. Sir, I know that well enough.

Val. What dost thou know?

Speed. That she is not so fair as, of you, well 55
favored.

Val. I mean that her beauty is exquisite but her
favor infinite.

Speed. That's because the one is painted and the
other out of all count. 60

Val. How painted? and how out of count?

Speed. Marry, sir, so painted, to make her fair, that
no man counts of her beauty.

Val. How esteemst thou me? I account of her
beauty. 65

Speed. You never saw her since she was deformed.

Val. How long hath she been deformed?

Speed. Ever since you loved her.

Val. I have loved her ever since I saw her, and still
I see her beautiful. 70

Speed. If you love her, you cannot see her.

Val. Why?

Speed. Because Love is blind. O, that you had mine
eyes, or your own eyes had the lights they were wont
to have when you chid at Sir Proteus for going un- 75
gartered!

Val. What should I see then?

Speed. Your own present folly and her passing de-
formity: for he, being in love, could not see to garter
his hose; and you, being in love, cannot see to put on 80
your hose.

Val. Belike, boy, then, you are in love, for last
morning you could not see to wipe my shoes.

85. **swinged:** beat.

88. **set:** (1) finished; (2) seated.

97–8. **motion:** a term applied to puppet and marionette shows. A secondary meaning, "idea" (Silvia's idea of the letter writing) is probably also intended. Valentine is a **puppet** being manipulated by Silvia.

104. **He should give her interest:** i.e., he is already interested in her.

Speed. True, sir: I was in love with my bed. I thank
you, you swinged me for my love, which makes me   85
the bolder to chide you for yours.

Val. In conclusion, I stand affected to her.

Speed. I would you were set, so your affection
would cease.

Val. Last night she enjoined me to write some   90
lines to one she loves.

Speed. And have you?

Val. I have.

Speed. Are they not lamely writ?

Val. No, boy, but as well as I can do them.   95
Peace! here she comes.

Speed. [*Aside*] O excellent motion! O exceeding
puppet! Now will he interpret to her.

[*Enter Silvia.*]

Val. Madam and mistress, a thousand good-mor-
rows.   100

Speed. [*Aside*] O, give ye good ev'n! here's a mil-
lion of manners.

Sil. Sir Valentine and servant, to you two thousand.

Speed. [*Aside*] He should give her interest, and she
gives it him.   105

Val. As you enjoined me, I have writ your letter
Unto the secret, nameless friend of yours;
Which I was much unwilling to proceed in,
But for my duty to your Ladyship.

Sil. I thank you, gentle servant: 'tis very clerkly 110
done.

117. **stead:** help.
120. **period:** conclusion.
128. **quaintly:** cleverly.
137. **so . . . so:** well and good . . . that's that.

MILA-   NESE.

A lady of Milan. From Cesare Vecellio, *Habiti antichi et moderni* (1590).

Val. Now trust me, madam, it came hardly off:
For, being ignorant to whom it goes,
I writ at random, very doubtfully.

    Sil. Perchance you think too much of so much 115
        pains?

    Val. No, madam, so it stead you, I will write,
Please you command, a thousand times as much:
And yet—

    Sil. A pretty period! Well, I guess the sequel;   120
And yet I will not name it—and yet I care not—
And yet take this again—and yet I thank you:
Meaning henceforth to trouble you no more.

    Speed. [*Aside*] And yet you will; and yet another
        "yet."   125

    Val. What means your Ladyship? Do you not like
        it?

    Sil. Yes, yes: the lines are very quaintly writ;
But since unwillingly, take them again.
Nay, take them.   130

    Val. Madam, they are for you.

    Sil. Ay, ay: you writ them, sir, at my request;
But I will none of them: they are for you.
I would have had them writ more movingly.

    Val. Please you, I'll write your Ladyship another.   135

    Sil. And when it's writ, for my sake read it over,
And if it please you, so; if not, why, so.

    Val. If it please me, madam, what then?

    Sil. Why, if it please you, take it for your labor:
And so, good morrow, servant.   *Exit Silvia.* 140

    Speed. O jest unseen, inscrutable, invisible,

156. **figure:** device.
165. **none:** no **earnest** (a down payment toward an agreed reward or fee).

As a nose on a man's face or a weathercock on a
    steeple!
My master sues to her; and she hath taught her suitor,
He being her pupil, to become her tutor.   145
O excellent device! was there ever heard a better,
That my master, being scribe, to himself should write
    the letter?

Val. How now, sir? What are you reasoning with
yourself?   150

Speed. Nay, I was rhyming: 'tis you that have the
reason.

Val. To do what?

Speed. To be a spokesman from Madam Silvia.

Val. To whom?   155

Speed. To yourself. Why, she woos you by a figure.

Val. What figure?

Speed. By a letter, I should say.

Val. Why, she hath not writ to me!

Speed. What need she, when she hath made you 160
write to yourself? Why, do you not perceive the jest?

Val. No, believe me.

Speed. No believing you, indeed, sir. But did you
perceive her earnest?

Val. She gave me none, except an angry word.   165

Speed. Why, she hath given you a letter.

Val. That's the letter I writ to her friend.

Speed. And that letter hath she delivered, and there
    an end.

Val. I would it were no worse.   170

Speed. I'll warrant you, 'tis as well:
For often have you writ to her; and she, in modesty,

178. **speak in print:** utter authoritatively.

181–82. **the chameleon Love can feed on the air:** the chameleon's diet of air was a popular misconception.

184. **moved:** persuaded (to go to dinner).

▬▬▬▬▬▬▬▬▬▬▬▬▬▬▬▬▬▬▬▬▬▬▬▬

II.ii. Proteus and Julia say farewell, exchanging rings as symbols of their faith.

▬▬▬▬▬▬▬▬▬▬▬▬▬▬▬▬

4. **turn:** alter in affection.

Or else for want of idle time, could not again reply;
Or fearing else some messenger, that might her mind
    discover,   175
Herself hath taught her love himself to write unto her
    lover.
All this I speak in print, for in print I found it. Why
muse you, sir? 'tis dinnertime.
    Val. I have dined.   180
    Speed. Ay, but hearken, sir; though the chameleon
Love can feed on the air, I am one that am nour-
ished by my victuals and would fain have meat. O,
be not like your mistress; be moved, be moved.

                                         Exeunt.

Scene II. [Verona. Julia's house.]

Enter Proteus and Julia.

    Pro. Have patience, gentle Julia.
    Jul. I must, where is no remedy.
    Pro. When possibly I can, I will return.
    Jul. If you turn not, you will return the sooner.
Keep this remembrance for thy Julia's sake.   5
                              Giving a ring.
    Pro. Why, then, we'll make exchange; here, take
    you this.
    Jul. And seal the bargain with a holy kiss.
    Pro. Here is my hand for my true constancy;
And when that hour o'erslips me in the day   10
Wherein I sigh not, Julia, for thy sake,

II.iii. Launce, Proteus' servant, has taken sorrowful leave of his family and deplores the fact that his dog has not shared the general grief. Panthino enters and urges him to hasten to the ship, which is ready to sail.

▬▬▬▬▬▬▬▬

2. **kind:** kindred; family.
3–4. **prodigious son:** the biblical prodigal son.

The next ensuing hour some foul mischance
Torment me for my love's forgetfulness!
My father stays my coming: answer not.
The tide is now—nay, not thy tide of tears;   15
That tide will stay me longer than I should.
Julia, farewell!   *Exit Julia.*
              What, gone without a word?
Ay, so true love should do: it cannot speak;
For truth hath better deeds than words to grace it.   20

[*Enter Panthino.*]

Pan. Sir Proteus, you are stayed for.
Pro. Go: I come, I come.
Alas! this parting strikes poor lovers dumb.
                            Exeunt.

Scene III. [Verona. A street.]

Enter Launce, [*leading a dog*].

Launce. Nay, 'twill be this hour ere I have done
weeping: all the kind of the Launces have this very
fault. I have received my proportion, like the prodigious son, and am going with Sir Proteus to the
Imperial's court. I think Crab, my dog, be the sourest-   5
natured dog that lives: my mother weeping, my father
wailing, my sister crying, our maid howling, our cat
wringing her hands, and all our house in a great per-
plexity, yet did not this cruel-hearted cur shed one

17. **the worser sole:** a pun on "soul," alluding to the belief held by some ancients that women have no souls.

27. **wood:** mad; probably with a pun on **wood** as the material of Launce's clogs.

29. **up and down:** exactly.

34. **post:** hurry.

tear. He is a stone, a very pebblestone, and has no   10
more pity in him than a dog. A Jew would have wept
to have seen our parting: why, my grandam, having no
eyes, look you, wept herself blind at my parting. Nay,
I'll show you the manner of it. This shoe is my father.
No, this left shoe is my father. No, no, this left shoe is   15
my mother. Nay, that cannot be so neither: yes, it is
so, it is so, it hath the worser sole. This shoe with the
hole in it is my mother and this my father: a venge-
ance on't! there 'tis. Now, sir, this staff is my sister, for,
look you, she is as white as a lily and as small as a   20
wand. This hat is Nan, our maid. I am the dog. No,
the dog is himself, and I am the dog. O! the dog is me,
and I am myself: ay, so, so. Now come I to my father:
"Father, your blessing." Now should not the shoe
speak a word for weeping: now should I kiss my   25
father; well, he weeps on. Now come I to my mother.
O, that she could speak now like a wood woman!
Well, I kiss her: why, there 'tis; here's my mother's
breath up and down. Now come I to my sister; mark
the moan she makes. Now the dog all this while sheds   30
not a tear nor speaks a word; but see how I lay the
dust with my tears.

[*Enter Panthino.*]

Pan. Launce, away, away, aboard! Thy master is
shipped, and thou art to post after with oars. What's
the matter? Why weepst thou, man? Away, ass! you'll   35
lose the tide, if you tarry any longer.

II.iv. Valentine, attending Silvia, is informed by the Duke that Proteus has arrived with high recommendations from great men. He confirms the good reports of his friend and greets Proteus warmly, beseeching Silvia to accept him as another follower. The two friends exchange news, Valentine singing the praises of Silvia, to whom he is now engaged. Proteus' one glimpse of Silvia has aroused his affection and he vows to himself to win her if he can, despite his friendship for Valentine.

Launce. It is no matter if the tied were lost; for it is the unkindest tied that ever any man tied.

Pan. What's the unkindest tide?

Launce. Why, he that's tied here, Crab, my dog. 40

Pan. Tut, man, I mean thou'lt lose the flood: and, in losing the flood, lose thy voyage, and, in losing thy voyage, lose thy master, and, in losing thy master, lose thy service, and, in losing thy service—Why dost thou stop my mouth? 45

Launce. For fear thou shouldst lose thy tongue.

Pan. Where should I lose my tongue?

Launce. In thy tale.

Pan. In thy tail!

Launce. Lose the tide, and the voyage, and the 50 master, and the service, and the tied! Why, man, if the river were dry, I am able to fill it with my tears; if the wind were down, I could drive the boat with my sighs.

Pan. Come, come away, man; I was sent to call thee. 55

Launce. Sir, call me what thou darest.

Pan. Wilt thou go?

Launce. Well, I will go.

Exeunt.

Scene IV. [Milan. The Duke's palace.]

Enter Valentine, Silvia, Thurio, and Speed.

Sil. Servant!

Val. Mistress?

18. **quote:** note.
22. **How:** an indignant exclamation.
24. **Give him leave:** pardon him.

Milan. From Pietro Bertelli, *Theatrum urbium Italicarum* (1597).

Speed. Master, Sir Thurio frowns on you.

Val. Ay, boy, it's for love.

Speed. Not of you. 5

Val. Of my mistress, then.

Speed. 'Twere good you knocked him. [*Exit.*]

Sil. Servant, you are sad.

Val. Indeed, madam, I seem so.

Thu. Seem you that you are not? 10

Val. Haply I do.

Thu. So do counterfeits.

Val. So do you.

Thu. What seem I that I am not?

Val. Wise. 15

Thu. What instance of the contrary?

Val. Your folly.

Thu. And how quote you my folly?

Val. I quote it in your jerkin.

Thu. My jerkin is a doublet. 20

Val. Well, then, I'll double your folly.

Thu. How!

Sil. What, angry, Sir Thurio! Do you change color?

Val. Give him leave, madam: he is a kind of chameleon. 25

Thu. That hath more mind to feed on your blood
than live in your air.

Val. You have said, sir.

Thu. Ay, sir, and done too, for this time.

Val. I know it well, sir: you always end ere you 30
begin.

Sil. A fine volley of words, gentlemen, and quickly
shot off.

38. kindly: naturally, properly (since she is its source).

43. liveries: uniforms.

52. happy messenger: bringer of happy news.

55. worthy estimation: honorable reputation.

Val. 'Tis indeed, madam, we thank the giver.

Sil. Who is that, servant?   35

Val. Yourself, sweet lady, for you gave the fire. Sir
Thurio borrows his wit from your Ladyship's looks
and spends what he borrows kindly in your company.

Thu. Sir, if you spend word for word with me, I
shall make your wit bankrupt.   40

Val. I know it well, sir: you have an exchequer of
words, and, I think, no other treasure to give your fol-
lowers, for it appears by their bare liveries that they
live by your bare words.

Sil. No more, gentlemen, no more: here comes my   45
father.

[Enter Duke.]

Duke. Now, daughter Silvia, you are hard beset.
Sir Valentine, your father is in good health:
What say you to a letter from your friends
Of much good news?   50

Val.   My lord, I will be thankful
To any happy messenger from thence.

Duke. Know ye Don Antonio, your countryman?

Val. Ay, my good lord, I know the gentleman
To be of worth and worthy estimation,   55
And not without desert so well reputed.

Duke. Hath he not a son?

Val. Ay, my good lord, a son that well deserves
The honor and regard of such a father.

Duke. You know him well?   60

Val. I know him as myself; for from our infancy

62. **conversed:** associated.
64. **Omitting:** neglecting.
72. **feature:** physical endowments.
74. **make this good:** confirm this.
84. **cite:** urge.
85. **presently:** at once.

We have conversed and spent our hours together;
And though myself have been an idle truant,
Omitting the sweet benefit of time
To clothe mine age with angel-like perfection,   65
Yet hath Sir Proteus, for that's his name,
Made use and fair advantage of his days;
His years but young, but his experience old;
His head unmellowed, but his judgment ripe;
And, in a word, for far behind his worth   70
Comes all the praises that I now bestow,
He is complete in feature and in mind,
With all good grace to grace a gentleman.
  Duke. Beshrew me, sir, but if he make this good,
He is as worthy for an empress' love   75
As meet to be an emperor's counselor.
Well, sir, this gentleman is come to me,
With commendation from great potentates;
And here he means to spend his time awhile.
I think 'tis no unwelcome news to you.   80
  Val. Should I have wished a thing, it had been he.
  Duke. Welcome him, then, according to his worth.
Silvia, I speak to you, and you, Sir Thurio,
For Valentine, I need not cite him to it.
I will send him hither to you presently   [*Exit.*]   85
  Val. This is the gentleman I told your Ladyship
Had come along with me but that his mistress
Did hold his eyes locked in her crystal looks.
  Sil. Belike that now she hath enfranchised them,
Upon some other pawn for fealty.   90
  Val. Nay, sure, I think she holds them prisoners still.
  Sil. Nay, then, he should be blind; and, being blind,

104. **entertain**: welcome.
112. **want**: lack.
114. **on**: i.e., in challenging.

How could he see his way to seek out you?
  Val. Why, lady, Love hath twenty pair of eyes.
  Thu. They say that Love hath not an eye at all.   95
  Val. To see such lovers, Thurio, as yourself:
Upon a homely object Love can wink.
  Sil. Have done, have done: here comes the gentle-
    man.

[Enter Proteus.]

  Val. Welcome, dear Proteus! Mistress, I beseech you, 100
Confirm his welcome with some special favor.
  Sil. His worth is warrant for his welcome hither,
If this be he you oft have wished to hear from.
  Val. Mistress, it is: sweet lady, entertain him
To be my fellow servant to your Ladyship.   105
  Sil. Too low a mistress for so high a servant.
  Pro. Not so, sweet lady; but too mean a servant
To have a look of such a worthy mistress.
  Val. Leave off discourse of disability:
Sweet lady, entertain him for your servant.   110
  Pro. My duty will I boast of, nothing else.
  Sil. And duty never yet did want his meed.
Servant, you are welcome to a worthless mistress.
  Pro. I'll die on him that says so but yourself.
  Sil. That you are welcome?   115
  Pro.   That you are worthless.

[Enter Servant.]

  Serv. Madam, my lord your father would speak
with you.

127–28. have them much commended: have sent many greetings.

145. to: compared with.

Sil. I wait upon his pleasure.   [*Exit Servant.*]
                                Come, Sir Thurio,   120
Go with me. Once more, new servant, welcome:
I'll leave you to confer of home affairs.
When you have done, we look to hear from you.
    Pro. We'll both attend upon your Ladyship.
                            [*Exeunt Silvia and Thurio.*]
    Val. Now, tell me, how do all from whence you   125
        came?
    Pro. Your friends are well and have them much
        commended.
    Val. And how do yours?
    Pro.   I left them all in health.   130
    Val. How does your lady? and how thrives your
        love?
    Pro. My tales of love were wont to weary you;
I know you joy not in a love discourse.
    Val. Ay, Proteus, but that life is altered now: 135
I have done penance for contemning Love,
Whose high imperious thoughts have punished me
With bitter fasts, with penitential groans,
With nightly tears, and daily heartsore sighs;
For, in revenge of my contempt of love,   140
Love hath chased sleep from my enthralled eyes
And made them watchers of mine own heart's sorrow.
O gentle Proteus, Love's a mighty lord
And hath so humbled me as I confess
There is no woe to his correction,   145
Nor to his service no such joy on earth.
Now no discourse, except it be of love:
Now can I break my fast, dine, sup, and sleep,

164. Except thou wilt except against my love: or you will depreciate my mistress.

166. prefer: advance; promote.

174. can: can say.

176. alone: incomparable.

As twenty seas, if all their sand were pearl,   180
The water nectar, and the rocks pure gold.
Forgive me that I do not dream on thee,
Because thou seest me dote upon my love.
My foolish rival, that her father likes
Only for his possessions are so huge,   185
Is gone with her along; and I must after,
For love, thou knowst, is full of jealousy.
   Pro. But she loves you?
   Val. Ay, and we are betrothed: nay, more, our mar-
     riage hour,   190
With all the cunning manner of our flight,
Determined of: how I must climb her window,
The ladder made of cords; and all the means
Plotted and 'greed on for my happiness.
Good Proteus, go with me to my chamber,   195
In these affairs to aid me with thy counsel.
   Pro. Go on before: I shall inquire you forth.
I must unto the road, to disembark
Some necessaries that I needs must use,
And then I'll presently attend you.   200
   Val. Will you make haste?
   Pro. I will.   *Exit* [*Valentine*].
Even as one heat another heat expels,
Or as one nail by strength drives out another,
So the remembrance of my former love   205
Is by a newer object quite forgotten.
Is it mine eye or Valentinus' praise,
Her true perfection, or my false transgression,
That makes me reasonless to reason thus?
She is fair, and so is Julia that I love—   210

218. **more advice:** further acquaintance.
220. **picture:** appearance.
223. **reason:** question.
225. **compass:** win.

IIIIIIIIIIIIIIIIIIIIIIIIIIIIIIIIIIIIIIIIIIIIIIIIIIIIII

II.v. A succession of quips between Launce and Speed.

IIIIIIIIIIIIIIIIIIIIIIIIIIIIIIIIIIII

5. **shot:** charge.

That I did love, for now my love is thawed;
Which, like a waxen image 'gainst a fire,
Bears no impression of the thing it was.
Methinks my zeal to Valentine is cold,
And that I love him not as I was wont.   215
O, but I love his lady too too much!
And that's the reason I love him so little.
How shall I dote on her with more advice,
That thus without advice begin to love her!
'Tis but her picture I have yet beheld,   220
And that hath dazzled my reason's light;
But when I look on her perfections,
There is no reason but I shall be blind.
If I can check my erring love, I will;
If not, to compass her I'll use my skill.   225

Exit.

Scene V. [Milan. A street.]

Enter Speed and Launce [severally].

Speed. Launce! by mine honesty, welcome to Milan!
Launce. Forswear not thyself, sweet youth; for I
am not welcome. I reckon this always, that a man is
never undone till he be hanged, nor never welcome to
a place till some certain shot be paid and the hostess   5
say "Welcome!"
Speed. Come on, you madcap, I'll to the alehouse
with you presently; where, for one shot of fivepence,

11. **closed in earnest:** embraced sincerely.

18. **as whole as a fish:** a proverbial expression (perhaps because fish have no limbs).

thou shalt have five thousand welcomes. But, sirrah,
how did thy master part with Madam Julia?   10

Launce. Marry, after they closed in earnest, they
parted very fairly in jest.

Speed. But shall she marry him?

Launce. No.

Speed. How, then? Shall he marry her?   15

Launce. No, neither.

Speed. What, are they broken?

Launce. No, they are both as whole as a fish.

Speed. Why, then, how stands the matter with
them?   20

Launce. Marry, thus: when it stands well with him,
it stands well with her.

Speed. What an ass art thou! I understand thee not.

Launce. What a block art thou that thou canst not!
My staff understands me.   25

Speed. What thou sayst?

Launce. Ay, and what I do too: look thee, I'll but
lean, and my staff understands me.

Speed. It stands under thee, indeed.

Launce. Why, stand under and understand is all   30
one.

Speed. But tell me true, will't be a match?

Launce. Ask my dog: if he say "ay," it will; if he say
"no," it will; if he shake his tail and say nothing, it
will.   35

Speed. The conclusion is, then, that it will.

Launce. Thou shalt never get such a secret from me
but by a parable.

Speed. 'Tis well that I get it so. But, Launce, how

45. **whoreson:** good-for-nothing.

55. **ale:** i.e., a parish **ale** or festival, at which funds were raised for church needs.

━━━━━━━━━━━━━━━━━━━━━━━━━━━━━━━

II.vi. Proteus muses on the predicament in which he finds himself. If he follows his heart and tries to win Silvia, he will be false to both Julia and Valentine. But he convinces himself that his love of Silvia is so overpowering that he must pursue it. Thus he justifies his intention of thwarting the elopement of Silvia and Valentine by revealing their plans to the Duke.

sayst thou that my master is become a notable lover?   40
Launce. I never knew him otherwise.
Speed. Than how?
Launce. A notable lubber, as thou reportest him to
be.
Speed. Why, thou whoreson ass, thou mistakest me.   45
Launce. Why fool, I meant not thee, I meant thy
master.
Speed. I tell thee, my master is become a hot lover.
Launce. Why, I tell thee, I care not though he burn
himself in love. If thou wilt, go with me to the ale-   50
house; if not, thou art an Hebrew, a Jew, and not
worth the name of a Christian.
Speed. Why?
Launce. Because thou hast not so much charity in
thee as to go to the ale with a Christian. Wilt thou   55
go?
Speed. At thy service.

Exeunt.

Scene VI. [Milan. The Duke's palace.]

Enter Proteus solus.

Pro. To leave my Julia, shall I be forsworn;
To love fair Silvia, shall I be forsworn;
To wrong my friend, I shall be much forsworn;
And even that power which gave me first my oath
Provokes me to this threefold perjury.   5
Love bade me swear, and Love bids me forswear.

7. **sweet-suggesting:** sweetly tempting.
12. **wants:** lacks.
13. **learn:** teach.
14. **unreverend:** disrespectful.
15. **preferred:** put forward; advanced.
17. **leave:** cease.
24. **still:** ever.
35. **competitor:** "ally," rather than "rival."
37. **pretended:** intended.

O sweet-suggesting Love, if thou hast sinned,
Teach me, thy tempted subject, to excuse it!
At first I did adore a twinkling star,
But now I worship a celestial sun.   10
Unheedful vows may heedfully be broken;
And he wants wit that wants resolved will
To learn his wit t'exchange the bad for better.
Fie, fie, unreverend tongue! to call her bad,
Whose sovereignty so oft thou hast preferred   15
With twenty thousand soul-confirming oaths.
I cannot leave to love, and yet I do;
But there I leave to love where I should love.
Julia I lose, and Valentine I lose:
If I keep them, I needs must lose myself;   20
If I lose them, thus find I by their loss,
For Valentine, myself; for Julia, Silvia.
I to myself am dearer than a friend,
For love is still most precious in itself;
And Silvia—witness Heaven, that made her fair!—   25
Shows Julia but a swarthy Ethiope.
I will forget that Julia is alive,
Rememb'ring that my love to her is dead;
And Valentine I'll hold an enemy,
Aiming at Silvia as a sweeter friend.   30
I cannot now prove constant to myself,
Without some treachery used to Valentine.
This night he meaneth with a corded ladder
To climb celestial Silvia's chamber window,
Myself in counsel, his competitor.   35
Now presently I'll give her father notice
Of their disguising and pretended flight;

41. blunt: stupid.

II.vii. Julia is desolate in Proteus' absence and asks Lucetta's assistance in attiring herself in masculine clothing to follow him. Lucetta warns her that she may not be welcome to her lover, but Julia is convinced of Proteus' constancy.

---

3. table: notebook.
4. charactered: written.
5. mean: means.
10. measure: tread from end to end.

Who, all enraged, will banish Valentine;
For Thurio he intends shall wed his daughter:
But, Valentine being gone, I'll quickly cross   40
By some sly trick blunt Thurio's dull proceeding.
Love, lend me wings to make my purpose swift,
As thou hast lent me wit to plot this drift!

                                                Exit.

Scene VII. [Verona. Julia's house.]

Enter Julia and Lucetta.

Jul. Counsel, Lucetta; gentle girl, assist me;
And, ev'n in kind love, I do conjure thee,
Who art the table wherein all my thoughts
Are visibly charactered and engraved,
To lesson me and tell me some good mean   5
How, with my honor, I may undertake
A journey to my loving Proteus.
  Luc. Alas, the way is wearisome and long!
  Jul. A true-devoted pilgrim is not weary
To measure kingdoms with his feeble steps;   10
Much less shall she that hath Love's wings to fly,
And when the flight is made to one so dear,
Of such divine perfection, as Sir Proteus.
  Luc. Better forbear till Proteus make return.
  Jul. Oh, knowst thou not his looks are my soul's   15
    food?
Pity the dearth that I have pined in,
By longing for that food so long a time.

19. **inly:** inwardly (and intensely) felt.
23. **qualify:** temper; moderate.
34. **sport:** playfulness.
41. **habit:** dress.
43. **loose encounters:** wanton solicitations.
44. **weeds:** garments.
45. **beseem:** become.
48. **odd-conceited:** quaintly contrived.

Didst thou but know the inly touch of love,
Thou wouldst as soon go kindle fire with snow   20
As seek to quench the fire of love with words.
    Luc. I do not seek to quench your love's hot fire,
But qualify the fire's extreme rage,
Lest it should burn above the bounds of reason.
    Jul. The more thou dammest it up, the more it   25
        burns.
The current that with gentle murmur glides,
Thou knowst, being stopped, impatiently doth rage;
But when his fair course is not hindered,
He makes sweet music with the enameled stones,   30
Giving a gentle kiss to every sedge
He overtaketh in his pilgrimage.
And so by many winding nooks he strays,
With willing sport, to the wild ocean.
Then let me go, and hinder not my course.   35
I'll be as patient as a gentle stream,
And make a pastime of each weary step,
Till the last step have brought me to my love;
And there I'll rest, as after much turmoil
A blessed soul doth in Elysium.   40
    Luc. But in what habit will you go along?
    Jul. Not like a woman, for I would prevent
The loose encounters of lascivious men.
Gentle Lucetta, fit me with such weeds
As may beseem some well-reputed page.   45
    Luc. Why, then, your Ladyship must cut your hair.
    Jul. No, girl, I'll knit it up in silken strings,
With twenty odd-conceited truelove knots.
To be fantastic may become a youth

50. **time:** age; **show:** seem.
53. **fits:** suits the occasion.
54. **farthingale:** hooped skirt.
59. **round hose:** breeches of a full, round shape.
65. **scandalized:** disgraced.
68. **dream on infamy:** consider disgrace.
74. **instances:** evidences; **infinite:** an infinity.
75. **Warrant:** assure.

Costume of an Italian youth. From Cesare Negri, *Nuove inventioni di balli* (1604).

Of greater time than I shall show to be.   50

  Luc. What fashion, madam, shall I make your
    breeches?

  Jul. That fits as well as, "Tell me, good my lord,
What compass will you wear your farthingale?"
Why ev'n what fashion thou best likes, Lucetta.   55

  Luc. You must needs have them with a codpiece,
    madam.

  Jul. Out, out, Lucetta! that will be ill-favored.

  Luc. A round hose, madam, now's not worth a pin,
Unless you have a codpiece to stick pins on.   60

  Jul. Lucetta, as thou lovest me, let me have
What thou thinkst meet and is most mannerly.
But tell me, wench, how will the world repute me
For undertaking so unstaid a journey?
I fear me, it will make me scandalized.   65

  Luc. If you think so, then stay at home and go not.

  Jul. Nay, that I will not.

  Luc. Then never dream on infamy, but go.
If Proteus like your journey when you come,
No matter who's displeased when you are gone: 70
I fear me, he will scarce be pleased withal.

  Jul. That is the least, Lucetta, of my fear:
A thousand oaths, an ocean of his tears,
And instances of infinite of love,
Warrant me welcome to my Proteus.   75

  Luc. All these are servants to deceitful men.

  Jul. Base men, that use them to so base effect!
But truer stars did govern Proteus' birth:
His words are bonds, his oaths are oracles;
His love sincere, his thoughts immaculate;   80

89. **take a note of:** consider.
90. **longing:** inspired by longing.
93. **dispatch me:** help me to a speedy departure.
95. **tarriance:** lingering.

His tears pure messengers sent from his heart;
His heart as far from fraud as Heaven from earth.
   Luc. Pray Heaven he prove so, when you come to
     him!
   Jul. Now, as thou lovest me, do him not that wrong   85
To bear a hard opinion of his truth.
Only deserve my love by loving him;
And presently go with me to my chamber,
To take a note of what I stand in need of
To furnish me upon my longing journey.   90
All that is mine I leave at thy dispose,
My goods, my lands, my reputation;
Only, in lieu thereof, dispatch me hence.
Come, answer not, but to it presently!
I am impatient of my tarriance.   95

                     Exeunt.

THE
TWO GENTLEMEN
OF
VERONA

ACT III

III.i. Proteus tells the Duke of his daughter's plan to elope with Valentine. When Valentine enters, the Duke tricks him into revealing a letter he has written to Silvia and the ladder of cords by which he means to rescue her from the tower in which she is locked at night. Since it is the Duke's intention for Silvia to marry Thurio, he sentences Valentine to banishment on pain of death.

━━━━━━━━━━━━━━━━━

1. **give us leave:** pardon us.
12. **privy to:** secretly informed of.
21. **timeless:** untimely.

ACT III

Scene I. [Milan. Without the Duke's palace.]

Enter Duke, Thurio, and Proteus.

Duke. Sir Thurio, give us leave, I pray, awhile:
We have some secrets to confer about. [*Exit Thurio.*]
Now, tell me, Proteus, what's your will with me?
   Pro. My gracious lord, that which I would discover
The law of friendship bids me to conceal;   5
But when I call to mind your gracious favors
Done to me, undeserving as I am,
My duty pricks me on to utter that
Which else no worldly good should draw from me.
Know, worthy prince, Sir Valentine, my friend,   10
This night intends to steal away your daughter:
Myself am one made privy to the plot.
I know you have determined to bestow her
On Thurio, whom your gentle daughter hates;
And should she thus be stol'n away from you,   15
It would be much vexation to your age.
Thus, for my duty's sake, I rather chose
To cross my friend in his intended drift
Than, by concealing it, heap on your head
A pack of sorrows, which would press you down,   20
Being unprevented, to your timeless grave.

41

28. **jealous aim:** suspicious guess.
34. **tender:** inexperienced; **suggested:** tempted.
45. **discovery:** disclosure; **aimed at:** suspected.
47. **pretense:** intention.

Duke. Proteus, I thank thee for thine honest care,
Which to requite, command me while I live.
This love of theirs myself have often seen,
Haply when they have judged me fast asleep,   25
And oftentimes have purposed to forbid
Sir Valentine her company and my court;
But, fearing lest my jealous aim might err,
And so, unworthily disgrace the man—
A rashness that I ever yet have shunned—   30
I gave him gentle looks, thereby to find
That which thyself hast now disclosed to me.
And, that thou mayst perceive my fear of this,
Knowing that tender youth is soon suggested,
I nightly lodge her in an upper tower,   35
The key whereof myself have ever kept;
And thence she cannot be conveyed away.
    Pro. Know, noble lord, they have devised a mean
How he her chamber window will ascend
And with a corded ladder fetch her down;   40
For which the youthful lover now is gone,
And this way comes he with it presently;
Where, if it please you, you may intercept him.
But, good my lord, do it so cunningly
That my discovery be not aimed at;   45
For, love of you, not hate unto my friend,
Hath made me publisher of this pretense.
    Duke. Upon mine honor, he shall never know
That I had any light from thee of this.
    Pro. Adieu, my lord: Sir Valentine is coming. [*Exit.*]   50

[*Enter Valentine.*]

59. **break with:** inform.

68. **peevish:** obstinate; **froward:** perverse.

73. **Upon advice:** after careful consideration of the matter.

81. **Verona:** Shakespeare was rather careless in references to places in this play. Some editors change to "Milano."

Duke. Sir Valentine, whither away so fast?
Val. Please it your Grace, there is a messenger
That stays to bear my letters to my friends,
And I am going to deliver them.
   Duke. Be they of much import?   55
Val. The tenor of them doth but signify
My health and happy being at your court.
   Duke. Nay then, no matter: stay with me awhile.
I am to break with thee of some affairs
That touch me near, wherein thou must be secret.   60
'Tis not unknown to thee that I have sought
To match my friend Sir Thurio to my daughter.
   Val. I know it well, my lord; and, sure, the match
Were rich and honorable; besides, the gentleman
Is full of virtue, bounty, worth, and qualities   65
Beseeming such a wife as your fair daughter.
Cannot your Grace win her to fancy him?
   Duke. No, trust me: she is peevish, sullen, froward,
Proud, disobedient, stubborn, lacking duty;
Neither regarding that she is my child,   70
Nor fearing me as if I were her father.
And, may I say to thee, this pride of hers,
Upon advice, hath drawn my love from her;
And, where I thought the remnant of mine age
Should have been cherished by her childlike duty,   75
I now am full resolved to take a wife,
And turn her out to who will take her in:
Then let her beauty be her wedding dower,
For me and my possessions she esteems not.
   Val. What would your Grace have me to do in this?   80
   Duke. There is a lady in Verona here

82. **affect:** love; **nice:** prim.
87. **bestow:** behave.
91. **quick:** lively.
100. **Forwhy:** because.

Whom I affect; but she is nice and coy
And nought esteems my aged eloquence.
Now, therefor would I have thee to my tutor—
For long agone I have forgot to court;   85
Besides, the fashion of the time is changed—
How and which way I may bestow myself
To be regarded in her sun-bright eye.
    Val. Win her with gifts, if she respect not words:
Dumb jewels often in their silent kind   90
More than quick words do move a woman's mind.
    Duke. But she did scorn a present that I sent her.
    Val. A woman sometime scorns what best contents
        her.
Send her another; never give her o'er: 95
For scorn at first makes after-love the more.
If she do frown, 'tis not in hate of you,
But rather to beget more love in you.
If she do chide, 'tis not to have you gone;
Forwhy the fools are mad if left alone.   100
Take no repulse, whatever she doth say:
For "get you gone," she doth not mean "away!"
Flatter and praise, commend, extol their graces;
Though ne'er so black, say they have angels' faces.
That man that hath a tongue, I say, is no man,   105
If with his tongue he cannot win a woman.
    Duke. But she I mean is promised by her friends
Unto a youthful gentleman of worth
And kept severely from resort of men,
That no man hath access by day to her.   110
    Val. Why, then, I would resort to her by night.

115. **lets:** prevents.
117. **shelving:** sloping.
118. **apparent:** certain.
119. **quaintly:** cleverly.
123. **blood:** breeding.
141. **engine:** contrivance (the rope ladder).

Duke. Ay, but the doors be locked and keys kept
    safe,
That no man hath recourse to her by night.
  Val. What lets but one may enter at her window?   115
  Duke. Her chamber is aloft, far from the ground,
And built so shelving that one cannot climb it
Without apparent hazard of his life.
  Val. Why, then, a ladder, quaintly made of cords,
To cast up, with a pair of anchoring hooks,   120
Would serve to scale another Hero's tower,
So bold Leander would adventure it.
  Duke. Now, as thou art a gentleman of blood,
Advise me where I may have such a ladder.
  Val. When would you use it? pray, sir, tell me that.   125
  Duke. This very night; for Love is like a child
That longs for everything that he can come by.
  Val. By seven o'clock I'll get you such a ladder.
  Duke. But, hark thee: I will go to her alone.
How shall I best convey the ladder thither?   130
  Val. It will be light, my lord, that you may bear it
Under a cloak that is of any length.
  Duke. A cloak as long as thine will serve the turn?
  Val. Ay, my good lord.
  Duke.   Then let me see thy cloak: 135
I'll get me one of such another length.
  Val. Why, any cloak will serve the turn, my lord.
  Duke. How shall I fashion me to wear a cloak?
I pray thee, let me feel thy cloak upon me.
What letter is this same? What's here? "To Silvia"!   140
And here an engine fit for my proceeding.
I'll be so bold to break the seal for once.   [*Reads*]

158. Phaeton: the son of Phoebus and Clymene. Merops was the latter's mortal husband. When Phaeton learned from his mother that his father was the sun-god, he demanded proof to convince his friends and would be satisfied with nothing less than the opportunity to drive his father's chariot of the sun. In Ovid's *Metamorphoses*, when Phaeton saw that his pride was going to result in his death, he regretted that he had not been content to be known as Merops' son.

162. overweening: presumptuous.

Phaeton. From Geoffrey Whitney, *Choice of Emblems* (1586).

"My thoughts do harbor with my Silvia nightly;
   And slaves they are to me, that send them flying:
O, could their master come and go as lightly,   145
   Himself would lodge where senseless they are
     lying!
My herald thoughts in thy pure bosom rest them;
   While I, their king, that thither them importune,
Do curse the grace that with such grace hath blessed 150
   them,
   Because myself do want my servants' fortune.
I curse myself, for they are sent by me,
That they should harbor where their lord should be."
What's here?   155
   "Silvia, this night I will enfranchise thee."
'Tis so; and here's the ladder for the purpose.
Why, Phaeton—for thou art Merops' son—
Wilt thou aspire to guide the heavenly car,
And with thy daring folly burn the world?   160
Wilt thou reach stars because they shine on thee?
Go, base intruder! overweening slave!
Bestow thy fawning smiles on equal mates;
And think my patience, more than thy desert,
Is privilege for thy departure hence.   165
Thank me for this more than for all the favors
Which, all too much, I have bestowed on thee.
But if thou linger in my territories
Longer than swiftest expedition
Will give thee time to leave our royal court,   170
By Heaven my wrath shall far exceed the love
I ever bore my daughter or thyself!
Be gone! I will not hear thy vain excuse;

187. **leave:** cease.
191. **attend on:** await.
194. **Soho:** a rallying cry to hound or hawk, urging the pursuit of the quarry.

But, as thou lovest thy life, make speed from hence.
                                        [*Exit.*]

Val. And why not death rather than living torment? 175
To die is to be banished from myself;
And Silvia is myself: banished from her
Is self from self: a deadly banishment!
What light is light, if Silvia be not seen?
What joy is joy, if Silvia be not by?   180
Unless it be to think that she is by,
And feed upon the shadow of perfection.
Except I be by Silvia in the night,
There is no music in the nightingale;
Unless I look on Silvia in the day,   185
There is no day for me to look upon:
She is my essence and I leave to be
If I be not by her fair influence
Fostered, illumined, cherished, kept alive.
I fly not death, to fly his deadly doom: 190
Tarry I here, I but attend on death;
But, fly I hence, I fly away from life.

[*Enter Proteus and Launce.*]

Pro. Run, boy, run, run, and seek him out.
Launce. Soho! Soho!
Pro. What seest thou?   195
Launce. Him we go to find:
There's not a hair on's head but 'tis a Valentine.
Pro. Valentine?
Val. No.
Pro. Who then? his spirit?   200

Val. Neither.

Pro. What then?

Val. Nothing.

Launce. Can nothing speak? Master, shall I strike?

Pro. Who wouldst thou strike?   205

Launce. Nothing.

Pro. Villain, forbear.

Launce. Why, sir, I'll strike nothing: I pray you—

Pro. Sirrah, I say, forbear! Friend Valentine,
    a word.   210

Val. My ears are stopped and cannot hear good
    news,
So much of bad already hath possessed them.

Pro. Then in dumb silence will I bury mine,
For they are harsh, untunable, and bad.   215

Val. Is Silvia dead?

Pro. No, Valentine.

Val. No Valentine, indeed, for sacred Silvia.
Hath she forsworn me?

Pro. No, Valentine.   220

Val. No Valentine, if Silvia have forsworn me.
What is your news?

Launce. Sir, there is a proclamation that you are
vanished.

Pro. That thou art banished—O, that's the news!— 225
From hence, from Silvia, and from me thy friend.

Val. O, I have fed upon this woe already,
And now excess of it will make me surfeit.
Doth Silvia know that I am banished?

Pro. Ay, ay; and she hath offered to the doom—   230
Which, unreversed, stands in effectual force—

233. **tendered:** offered.
242. **repeal:** recall.
256. **manage:** wield (like a weapon).
260. **The time now serves not to expostulate:** this is no moment to voice your complaints.
262. **at large:** fully.

A sea of melting pearl, which some call tears:
Those at her father's churlish feet she tendered;
With them, upon her knees, her humble self,
Wringing her hands, whose whiteness so became them 235
As if but now they waxed pale for woe.
But neither bended knees, pure hands held up,
Sad sighs, deep groans, nor silver-shedding tears
Could penetrate her uncompassionate sire;
But Valentine, if he be ta'en, must die.   240
Besides, her intercession chafed him so,
When she for thy repeal was suppliant,
That to close prison he commanded her,
With many bitter threats of biding there.

   Val. No more, unless the next word that thou 245
     speakst
Have some malignant power upon my life:
If so, I pray thee, breathe it in mine ear,
As ending anthem of my endless dolor.

   Pro. Cease to lament for that thou canst not help, 250
And study help for that which thou lamentst.
Time is the nurse and breeder of all good.
Here, if thou stay, thou canst not see thy love;
Besides, thy staying will abridge thy life.
Hope is a lover's staff: walk hence with that   255
And manage it against despairing thoughts.
Thy letters may be here, though thou art hence;
Which, being writ to me, shall be delivered
Even in the milk-white bosom of thy love.
The time now serves not to expostulate: 260
Come, I'll convey thee through the city gate;
And, ere I part with thee, confer at large

277. **gossips:** godparents (for a bastard child).
280. **bare:** mere.
281. **cate-log:** description of his sweetheart, whose name, presumably, is Kate; **Imprimis:** first of all.
284. **jade:** (1) nag; (2) minx.

Of all that may concern thy love affairs.
As thou lovest Silvia, though not for thyself,
Regard thy danger, and along with me!   265

   Val. I pray thee, Launce, and if thou seest my boy,
Bid him make haste and meet me at the north gate.

   Pro. Go, sirrah, find him out. Come, Valentine.

   Val. O, my dear Silvia! Hapless Valentine!

               [Exeunt Valentine and Proteus.]

   Launce. I am but a fool, look you; and yet I have   270
the wit to think my master is a kind of a knave: but
that's all one, if he be but one knave. He lives not now
that knows me to be in love, yet I am in love; but a
team of horses shall not pluck that from me, nor who
'tis I love. And yet 'tis a woman; but what woman I   275
will not tell myself. And yet 'tis a milkmaid; yet 'tis
not a maid, for she hath had gossips. Yet 'tis a maid,
for she is her master's maid and serves for wages. She
hath more qualities than a water spaniel, which is
much in a bare Christian. *[Pulling out a paper.]* Here   280
is the cate-log of her condition. "*Imprimis:* She can
fetch and carry." Why, a horse can do no more. Nay, a
horse cannot fetch, but only carry; therefore is she
better than a jade. "Item: She can milk"; look you, a
sweet virtue in a maid with clean hands.   285

               [Enter Speed.]

   Speed. How now, Signior Launce! what news with
your mastership?

   Launce. With my master's ship? Why, it is at sea.

295. **jolthead:** blockhead.

299. **Marry:** verily; originally, "by the Virgin Mary."

300. **loiterer:** truant.

303. **St. Nicholas:** patron saint of scholars; **be thy speed:** assist thee.

312. **stock:** dowry.

313. **stock:** stocking.

318. **set the world on wheels:** get ahead in the world with ease.

Illustration to *The World Runs on Wheels* by John Taylor. From *All the Works of John Taylor* (1630).

Speed. Well, your old vice still, mistake the word.
What news, then, in your paper?   290
Launce. The blackest news that ever thou heardst.
Speed. Why, man, how black?
Launce. Why, as black as ink.
Speed. Let me read them.
Launce. Fie on thee, jolthead! thou canst not read.   295
Speed. Thou liest; I can.
Launce. I will try thee. Tell me this: who begot
thee?
Speed. Marry, the son of my grandfather.
Launce. O illiterate loiterer! It was the son of thy   300
grandmother: this proves that thou canst not read.
Speed. Come, fool, come: try me in thy paper.
Launce. There; and St. Nicholas be thy speed!
Speed. [*Reads*] "Imprimis: She can milk."
Launce. Ay, that she can.   305
Speed. "Item: She brews good ale."
Launce. And thereof comes the proverb: "Blessing
of your heart, you brew good ale."
Speed. "Item: She can sew."
Launce. That's as much as to say, "Can she so?"   310
Speed. "Item: She can knit."
Launce. What need a man care for a stock with a
wench, when she can knit him a stock?
Speed. "Item: She can wash and scour."
Launce. A special virtue; for then she need not be   315
washed and scoured.
Speed. "Item: She can spin."
Launce. Then may I set the world on wheels, when
she can spin for her living.

326. fasting: popularly believed to cause bad breath.

333–34. sleep . . . in her talk: talk thoughtlessly.

345. curst: shrewish.

350. liberal: generous.

Speed. "Item: She hath many nameless virtues."   320

Launce. That's as much as to say, bastard virtues, that indeed know not their fathers and therefore have no names.

Speed. "Here follow her vices."

Launce. Close at the heels of her virtues.   325

Speed. "Item: She is not to be kissed fasting, in respect of her breath."

Launce. Well, that fault may be mended with a breakfast. Read on.

Speed. "Item: She hath a sweet mouth."   330

Launce. That makes amends for her sour breath.

Speed. "Item: She doth talk in her sleep."

Launce. It's no matter for that, so she sleep not in her talk.

Speed. "Item: She is slow in words."   335

Launce. O villain, that set this down among her vices! To be slow in words is a woman's only virtue: I pray thee, out with 't and place it for her chief virtue.

Speed. "Item: She is proud."

Launce. Out with that too: it was Eve's legacy and   340
cannot be ta'en from her.

Speed. "Item: She hath no teeth."

Launce. I care not for that neither, because I love crusts.

Speed. "Item: She is curst."   345

Launce. Well, the best is, she hath no teeth to bite.

Speed. "Item: She will often praise her liquor."

Launce. If her liquor be good, she shall: if she will not, I will; for good things should be praised.

Speed. "Item: She is too liberal."   350

369. gracious: graced.

Launce. Of her tongue she cannot, for that's writ down she is slow of; of her purse she shall not, for that I'll keep shut; now, of another thing she may, and that cannot I help. Well, proceed.

Speed. "Item: She hath more hair than wit, and 355 more faults than hairs, and more wealth than faults."

Launce. Stop there: I'll have her. She was mine, and not mine, twice or thrice in that last article. Rehearse that once more.

Speed. "Item: She hath more hair than wit."   360

Launce. More hair than wit? It may be: I'll prove it. The cover of the salt hides the salt, and therefore it is more than the salt; the hair that covers the wit is more than the wit, for the greater hides the less. What's next?   365

Speed. "And more faults than hairs."

Launce. That's monstrous: O, that that were out!

Speed. "And more wealth than faults."

Launce. Why, that word makes the faults gracious. Well, I'll have her: and if it be a match, as nothing is 370 impossible—

Speed. What then?

Launce. Why then will I tell thee that thy master stays for thee at the north gate.

Speed. For me?   375

Launce. For thee! Ay, who art thou? He hath stayed for a better man than thee.

Speed. And must I go to him?

Launce. Thou must run to him, for thou hast stayed so long that going will scarce serve the turn.   380

III.ii. The Duke assures Thurio that Silvia, with Valentine away, will return his love. He consults Proteus about a means of persuading Silvia to favor Thurio. Proteus advises him to have Valentine slandered to turn her love away from him and reveals himself as willing to be the disparager of his friend on Thurio's behalf. He counsels Thurio to serenade Silvia by night and at the latter's request goes with him to assemble a company of musicians.

7. **Trenched:** incised.
8. **his:** its.

Speed. Why didst not tell me sooner? 'Pox of your love letters!   [*Exit.*]

Launce. Now will he be swinged for reading my letter—an unmannerly slave, that will thrust himself into secrets! I'll after, to rejoice in the boy's correc- 385 tion.

                                                    Exit.

Scene II. [Milan. The Duke's palace.]

Enter Duke and Thurio.

Duke. Sir Thurio, fear not but that she will love you
Now Valentine is banished from her sight.
Thu. Since his exile she hath despised me most,
Forsworn my company, and railed at me,
That I am desperate of obtaining her.   5
Duke. This weak impress of love is as a figure
Trenched in ice, which, with an hour's heat,
Dissolves to water and doth lose his form.
A little time will melt her frozen thoughts,
And worthless Valentine shall be forgot.   10

[*Enter Proteus.*]

How now, Sir Proteus! Is your countryman,
According to our proclamation, gone?
Pro. Gone, my good lord.
Duke. My daughter takes his going grievously.
Pro. A little time, my lord, will kill that grief.   15

17. **conceit:** opinion.
36. **circumstance:** circumstantial (corroborative) detail.
41. **very:** true; undoubted.
44. **indifferent:** of no consequence.

Duke. So I believe; but Thurio thinks not so.
Proteus, the good conceit I hold of thee—
For thou hast shown some sign of good desert—
Makes me the better to confer with thee.

Pro. Longer than I prove loyal to your Grace   20
Let me not live to look upon your Grace.

Duke. Thou knowst how willingly I would effect
The match between Sir Thurio and my daughter?

Pro. I do, my lord.

Duke. And also, I think, thou art not ignorant   25
How she opposes her against my will.

Pro. She did, my lord, when Valentine was here.

Duke. Ay, and perversely she persevers so.
What might we do to make the girl forget
The love of Valentine and love Sir Thurio?   30

Pro. The best way is to slander Valentine
With falsehood, cowardice and poor descent,
Three things that women highly hold in hate.

Duke. Ay, but she'll think that it is spoke in hate.

Pro. Ay, if his enemy deliver it: 35
Therefore it must with circumstance be spoken
By one whom she esteemeth as his friend.

Duke. Then you must undertake to slander him.

Pro. And that, my lord, I shall be loath to do:
'Tis an ill office for a gentleman,   40
Especially against his very friend.

Duke. Where your good word cannot advantage him,
Your slander never can endamage him;
Therefore the office is indifferent,
Being entreated to it by your friend.   45

Pro. You have prevailed, my lord: if I can do it

53. provide: be careful; **bottom:** the core of a spool of thread was called a **bottom.**

68. lime: a glue used to trap birds.

70. full fraught: fully laden.

77. integrity: heartfelt sincerity.

By aught that I can speak in his dispraise,
She shall not long continue love to him.
But say this weed her love from Valentine,
It follows not that she will love Sir Thurio.   50

   Thu. Therefore, as you unwind her love from him,
Lest it should ravel and be good to none,
You must provide to bottom it on me;
Which must be done by praising me as much
As you in worth dispraise Sir Valentine.   55

   Duke. And, Proteus, we dare trust you in this kind,
Because we know, on Valentine's report,
You are already Love's firm votary
And cannot soon revolt and change your mind.
Upon this warrant shall you have access   60
Where you with Silvia may confer at large;
For she is lumpish, heavy, melancholy,
And, for your friend's sake, will be glad of you;
Where you may temper her by your persuasion
To hate young Valentine and love my friend.   65

   Pro. As much as I can do, I will effect:
But you, Sir Thurio, are not sharp enough;
You must lay lime to tangle her desires
By wailful sonnets, whose composed rhymes
Should be full fraught with serviceable vows.   70

   Duke. Ay,
Much is the force of Heaven-bred poesy.

   Pro. Say that upon the altar of her beauty
You sacrifice your tears, your sighs, your heart.
Write till your ink be dry, and with your tears   75
Moist it again; and frame some feeling line
That may discover such integrity:

81. **unsounded:** immeasurable.
84. **consort:** musical ensemble.
85. **dump:** doleful tune.
86. **grievance:** expression of grief.
87. **inherit:** obtain.
88. **discipline:** course of instruction.
92. **sort:** select.
94. **onset:** beginning.
97. **determine:** conclude.

Orpheus charming the beasts. From Ovid, *Metamorphoses* (1509).

For Orpheus' lute was strung with poets' sinews;
Whose golden touch could soften steel and stones,
Make tigers tame and huge leviathans   80
Forsake unsounded deeps to dance on sands.
After your dire-lamenting elegies,
Visit by night your lady's chamber window
With some sweet consort: to their instruments
Tune a deploring dump. The night's dead silence   85
Will well become such sweet-complaining grievance.
This, or else nothing, will inherit her.
   Duke. This discipline shows thou hast been in love.
   Thu. And thy advice this night I'll put in practice.
Therefore, sweet Proteus, my direction giver,   90
Let us into the city presently
To sort some gentlemen well skilled in music.
I have a sonnet that will serve the turn
To give the onset to thy good advice.
   Duke. About it, gentlemen!   95
   Pro. We'll wait upon your Grace till after supper,
And afterward determine our proceedings.
   Duke. Even now about it! I will pardon you.
                                      Exeunt.

THE
TWO GENTLEMEN
OF
VERONA

ACT IV

IV.i. Valentine, in flight from Milan, is taken by a band of outlaws. His appearance and behavior so impress them that they urge him to become their leader. All have been outlawed for minor offenses and are gentlemen rather than ruffians. Valentine agrees to join them on condition that they do not harm weak and defenseless travelers.

12. **proper:** fine, in the sense "manly."

ACT IV

Scene I. [The frontiers of Mantua. A forest.]

Enter Certain Outlaws.

1. Out. Fellows, stand fast: I see a passenger.
2. Out. If there be ten, shrink not, but down with
'em.

[*Enter Valentine and Speed.*]

3. Out. Stand, sir, and throw us that you have about
    ye: 5
If not, we'll make you sit and rifle you.
Speed. Sir, we are undone. These are the villains
That all the travelers do fear so much.
Val. My friends—
1. Out. That's not so, sir: we are your enemies.   10
2. Out. Peace! we'll hear him.
3. Out. Ay, by my beard, will we, for he is a proper
man.
Val. Then know that I have little wealth to lose:
A man I am crossed with adversity.   15
My riches are these poor habiliments,
Of which, if you should here disfurnish me,
You take the sum and substance that I have.

26. **crooked:** adverse.

46. **take to:** fall back on for subsistence.

47. **fortune:** i.e., the destiny, good or bad, that may be in store for him.

2. *Out.* Whither travel you?

Val. To Verona.   20

1. *Out.* Whence came you?

Val. From Milan.

3. *Out.* Have you long sojourned there?

Val. Some sixteen months, and longer might have
   stayed,   25
If crooked fortune had not thwarted me.

1. *Out.* What, were you banished thence?

Val. I was.

2. *Out.* For what offense?

Val. For that which now torments me to rehearse: 30
I killed a man, whose death I much repent;
But yet I slew him manfully in fight,
Without false vantage or base treachery.

1. *Out.* Why, ne'er repent it, if it were done so.
But were you banished for so small a fault?   35

Val. I was, and held me glad of such a doom.

2. *Out.* Have you the tongues?

Val. My youthful travail therein made me happy,
Or else I often had been miserable.

3. *Out.* By the bare scalp of Robin Hood's fat friar, 40
This fellow were a king for our wild faction!

1. *Out.* We'll have him. Sirs, a word.

Speed. Master, be one of them: it's an honorable
   kind of thievery.

Val. Peace, villain!   45

2. *Out.* Tell us this: have you anything to take to?

Val. Nothing but my fortune.

3. *Out.* Know, then, that some of us are gentlemen,
Such as the fury of ungoverned youth

50. **awful men:** men who are awed by order and authority and conform to the law.
52. **practicing:** plotting.
53. **allied:** related.
61. **perfection:** accomplishment.
62. **quality:** profession.
64. **parley:** offer terms.
68–9. **consort:** company.
78. **silly:** defenseless; **passengers:** travelers.

Thrust from the company of awful men: 50
Myself was from Verona banished
For practicing to steal away a lady,
An heir and near allied unto the Duke.
   2. Out. And I from Mantua, for a gentleman,
Who, in my mood, I stabbed unto the heart.   55
   1. Out. And I for suchlike petty crimes as these.
But to the purpose—for we cite our faults,
That they may hold excused our lawless lives;
And partly, seeing you are beautified
With goodly shape, and by your own report   60
A linguist and a man of such perfection
As we do in our quality much want—
   2. Out. Indeed, because you are a banished man,
Therefore, above the rest, we parley to you:
Are you content to be our general?   65
To make a virtue of necessity
And live, as we do, in this wilderness?
   3. Out. What sayst thou? Wilt thou be of our consort?
Say ay, and be the captain of us all.   70
We'll do thee homage and be ruled by thee,
Love thee as our commander and our king.
   1. Out. But if thou scorn our courtesy, thou diest.
   2. Out. Thou shalt not live to brag what we have
    offered.   75
   Val. I take your offer and will live with you,
Provided that you do no outrages
On silly women or poor passengers.
   3. Out. No, we detest such vile, base practices.
Come, go with us, we'll bring thee to our crews   80

IV.ii. Proteus has preceded Thurio to Silvia's window to urge his own suit. Thurio suspects his motives but is reassured by Proteus that he only acts for him. The disguised Julia enters unnoticed in the midst of the serenade and is grieved to see Proteus wooing another woman. When Silvia reproaches Proteus for breaking his oath to Julia, he tells her that Julia is dead. Silvia is unmoved by his protestations but agrees to let him have her picture. She feels that a woman's mere likeness is a suitable object of love for a man so lacking in sincerity.

▬▬▬▬▬▬▬▬▬▬▬▬▬

3. **color:** pretense.
12. **sudden:** sharp.

And show thee all the treasure we have got;
Which, with ourselves, all rest at thy dispose.

                                                Exeunt.

Scene II. [Milan. Outside Silvia's chamber.]

Enter Proteus.

Pro. Already have I been false to Valentine,
And now I must be as unjust to Thurio.
Under the color of commending him,
I have access my own love to prefer:
But Silvia is too fair, too true, too holy,   5
To be corrupted with my worthless gifts.
When I protest true loyalty to her,
She twits me with my falsehood to my friend.
When to her beauty I commend my vows,
She bids me think how I have been forsworn   10
In breaking faith with Julia whom I loved;
And, notwithstanding all her sudden quips,
The least whereof would quell a lover's hope,
Yet, spaniel-like, the more she spurns my love,
The more it grows and fawneth on her still.   15
But here comes Thurio: now must we to her window
And give some evening music to her ear.

[*Enter Thurio and Musicians.*]

Thu. How now, Sir Proteus, are you crept before us?
Pro. Ay, gentle Thurio, for you know that love

20. **go:** walk upright.
27–8. **allicholly:** melancholy.

Will creep in service where it cannot go.   20
   Thu. Ay, but I hope, sir, that you love not here.
   Pro. Sir, but I do: or else I would be hence.
   Thu. Who? Silvia?
   Pro. Ay, Silvia, for your sake.
   Thu. I thank you for your own. Now, gentlemen,   25
Let's tune, and to it lustily awhile.

[*Enter, at a distance, Host, and Julia in boy's clothes.*]

   Host. Now, my young guest, methinks you're alli-
     cholly: I pray you, why is it?
   Jul. Marry, mine host, because I cannot be merry.
   Host. Come, we'll have you merry. I'll bring you   30
where you shall hear music and see the gentleman
that you asked for.
   Jul. But shall I hear him speak?
   Host. Ay, that you shall.
   Jul. That will be music.   [*Music plays.*]   35
   Host. Hark, hark!
   Jul. Is he among these?
   Host. Ay: but, peace! let's hear 'em.

Song.

   Who is Silvia? what is she,
     That all our swains commend her?   40
   Holy, fair, and wise is she,
     The Heaven such grace did lend her,
   That she might admired be.

45. beauty lives with kindness: cf. the proverb "Handsome is as handsome does."

55. likes: pleases.

67. change: variation.

72. on: of.

Is she kind as she is fair?
   For beauty lives with kindness.   45
Love doth to her eyes repair,
   To help him of his blindness,
And, being helped, inhabits there.

Then to Silvia let us sing,
   That Silvia is excelling.   50
She excels each mortal thing
   Upon the dull earth dwelling:
To her let us garlands bring.

Host. How now! are you sadder than you were before? How do you, man? The music likes you not.   55

Jul. You mistake: the musician likes me not.

Host. Why, my pretty youth?

Jul. He plays false, father.

Host. How? out of tune on the strings?

Jul. Not so; but yet so false that he grieves my very   60
heartstrings.

Host. You have a quick ear.

Jul. Ay, I would I were deaf: it makes me have a
slow heart.

Host. I perceive you delight not in music.   65

Jul. Not a whit, when it jars so.

Host. Hark, what fine change is in the music!

Jul. Ay, that change is the spite.

Host. You would have them always play but one
thing?   70

Jul. I would always have one play but one thing.
But, host, doth this Sir Proteus that we talk on

75. out of all nick: beyond reckoning. Tavern accounts were kept by notches (nicks) on a stick.

94. compass: achieve.

97. subtle: crafty; underhanded.

98. conceitless: lacking in shrewdness.

64

Often resort unto this gentlewoman?

Host. I tell you what Launce, his man, told me: he
loved her out of all nick.   75

Jul. Where is Launce?

Host. Gone to seek his dog, which tomorrow, by his
master's command, he must carry for a present to his
lady.

Jul. Peace! stand aside: the company parts.   80

Pro. Sir Thurio, fear not you: I will so plead,
That you shall say my cunning drift excels.

Thu. Where meet we?

Pro.   At St. Gregory's well.

Thu.   Farewell.   85

         [Exeunt Thurio and Musicians.]

           [Enter Silvia above.]

Pro. Madam, good even to your Ladyship.

Sil. I thank you for your music, gentlemen.
Who is that that spake?

Pro. One, lady, if you knew his pure heart's truth,
You would quickly learn to know him by his voice.   90

Sil. Sir Proteus, as I take it.

Pro. Sir Proteus, gentle lady, and your servant.

Sil. What's your will?

Pro.   That I may compass yours.

Sil. You have your wish. My will is even this: 95
That presently you hie you home to bed.
Thou subtle, perjured, false, disloyal man!
Thinkst thou I am so shallow, so conceitless,
To be seduced by thy flattery,

102. queen of night: the moon.

That hast deceived so many with thy vows?   100
Return, return, and make thy love amends.
For me—by this pale queen of night I swear—
I am so far from granting thy request,
That I despise thee for thy wrongful suit
And by and by intend to chide myself   105
Even for this time I spend in talking to thee.
　　Pro. I grant, sweet love, that I did love a lady;
But she is dead.
　　Jul. [*Aside*] 'Twere false, if I should speak it;
For I am sure she is not buried.   110
　　Sil. Say that she be; yet Valentine thy friend
Survives, to whom, thyself art witness,
I am betrothed; and art thou not ashamed
To wrong him with thy importunacy?
　　Pro. I likewise hear that Valentine is dead.   115
　　Sil. And so suppose am I; for in his grave
Assure thyself my love is buried.
　　Pro. Sweet lady, let me rake it from the earth.
　　Sil. Go to thy lady's grave and call hers thence;
Or, at the least, in hers sepulcher thine.   120
　　Jul. [*Aside*] He heard not that.
　　Pro. Madam, if your heart be so obdurate,
Vouchsafe me yet your picture for my love,
The picture that is hanging in your chamber.
To that I'll speak, to that I'll sigh and weep: 125
For since the substance of your perfect self
Is else devoted, I am but a shadow,
And to your shadow will I make true love.
　　Jul. [*Aside*] If 'twere a substance, you would, sure,
　　　deceive it   130

140. **halidom:** literally, "holiness," or "holy relic."
145. **most heaviest:** saddest. Double superlatives were not uncommon in Elizabethan usage.

━━━━━━━━━━━━━━━━━━━━━━━━━━━━━━━━

IV.iii. Silvia has summoned Eglamour and asks him to help her escape and find her way to Valentine. Eglamour agrees to accompany her and they arrange to meet that evening at the cell of Friar Patrick.

And make it but a shadow, as I am.

Sil. I am very loath to be your idol, sir;
But since your falsehood shall become you well
To worship shadows and adore false shapes,
Send to me in the morning and I'll send it.   135
And so, good rest.

Pro.   As wretches have o'ernight
That wait for execution in the morn.

    [*Exeunt Proteus and Silvia, severally.*]

Jul. Host, will you go?

Host. By my halidom, I was fast asleep.   140

Jul. Pray you, where lies Sir Proteus?

Host. Marry, at my house. Trust me, I think 'tis almost day.

Jul. Not so; but it hath been the longest night
That e'er I watched, and the most heaviest.   145

        Exeunt.

Scene III. [Milan. Outside the Duke's palace.]

Enter Eglamour.

Egla. This is the hour that Madam Silvia
Entreated me to call and know her mind:
There's some great matter she'd employ me in.
Madam, madam!

    [*Enter Silvia above.*]

Sil.   Who calls?   5

Egla.   Your servant and your friend;

10. **impose:** order; request.
15. **remorseful:** compassionate.
19. **Vain:** worthless.
26. **for:** because.
33. **still:** ever.

One that attends your Ladyship's command.
   Sil. Sir Eglamour, a thousand times good morrow.
   Egla. As many, worthy lady, to yourself.
According to your Ladyship's impose,   10
I am thus early come to know what service
It is your pleasure to command me in.
   Sil. O Eglamour, thou art a gentleman—
Think not I flatter, for I swear I do not—
Valiant, wise, remorseful, well accomplished.   15
Thou art not ignorant what dear good will
I bear unto the banished Valentine,
Nor how my father would enforce me marry
Vain Thurio, whom my very soul abhors.
Thyself hast loved; and I have heard thee say   20
No grief did ever come so near thy heart
As when thy lady and thy true love died,
Upon whose grave thou vowedst pure chastity.
Sir Eglamour, I would to Valentine,
To Mantua, where I hear he makes abode;   25
And, for the ways are dangerous to pass,
I do desire thy worthy company,
Upon whose faith and honor I repose.
Urge not my father's anger, Eglamour,
But think upon my grief, a lady's grief,   30
And on the justice of my flying hence,
To keep me from a most unholy match,
Which Heaven and Fortune still rewards with plagues.
I do desire thee, even from a heart
As full of sorrows as the sea of sands,   35
To bear me company and go with me:
If not, to hide what I have said to thee,

42. Recking: heeding.

▬▬▬▬▬▬▬▬▬▬▬▬▬▬▬▬▬

IV.iv. Julia, calling herself Sebastian, has gáined entrance to Proteus and secured employment as a page. The first service he asks of her is to carry a ring to Silvia as a token of love and obtain in exchange the picture that Silvia has promised. Julia recognizes the ring she gave Proteus as a pledge but dutifully carries it to Silvia. Silvia knows the history of the ring, comforts Julia, and refuses to accept the token, although she sends her picture.

▬▬▬▬▬▬▬▬▬▬▬▬▬▬▬

10. keep: behave.

That I may venture to depart alone.

Egla. Madam, I pity much your grievances;
Which since I know they virtuously are placed,   40
I give consent to go along with you;
Recking as little what betideth me
As much I wish all good befortune you.
When will you go?

Sil.   This evening coming.   45

Egla. Where shall I meet you?

Sil.   At Friar Patrick's cell,
Where I intend holy confession.

Egla. I will not fail your Ladyship. Good morrow,
    gentle lady.   50

Sil. Good morrow, kind Sir Eglamour.

                                              [*Exeunt.*]

Scene IV. [Milan. Outside the Duke's palace.]

Enter Launce, [with his dog].

Launce. When a man's servant shall play the cur
with him, look you, it goes hard: one that I brought
up of a puppy; one that I saved from drowning, when
three or four of his blind brothers and sisters went to
it! I have taught him, even as one would say precisely: 5
"Thus I would teach a dog." I was sent to deliver him
as a present to Mistress Silvia from my master; and I
came no sooner into the dining chamber but he steps
me to her trencher and steals her capon's leg. O, 'tis a
foul thing when a cur cannot keep himself in all com-   10

11–12. **takes upon him:** pretends.

12. **a dog:** i.e., an expert.

18. **bless the mark:** a conventional apology for the offensive word that follows.

27. **wot:** know.

panies! I would have, as one should say, one that takes
upon him to be a dog indeed, to be, as it were, a dog
at all things. If I had not had more wit than he, to
take a fault upon me that he did, I think verily he had
been hanged for't; sure as I live, he had suffered for't: 15
you shall judge. He thrusts me himself into the company of three or four gentleman-like dogs under the
Duke's table: he had not been there—bless the mark!
—a pissing while, but all the chamber smelt him. "Out
with the dog!" says one. "What cur is that?" says an-   20
other. "Whip him out," says the third. "Hang him up,"
says the Duke. I, having been acquainted with the
smell before, knew it was Crab and goes me to the
fellow that whips the dogs. "Friend," quoth I, "you
mean to whip the dog!" "Ay, marry, do I," quoth he.   25
"You do him the more wrong," quoth I; "'twas I did
the thing you wot of." He makes me no more ado but
whips me out of the chamber. How many masters
would do this for his servant? Nay, I'll be sworn, I
have sat in the stocks for puddings he hath stol'n,   30
otherwise he had been executed. I have stood on the
pillory for geese he hath killed, otherwise he had suffered for't. Thou thinkst not of this now. Nay, I remember the trick you served me when I took my leave
of Madam Silvia: did not I bid thee still mark me and   35
do as I do? When didst thou see me heave up my leg
and make water against a gentlewoman's farthingale?
Didst thou ever see me do such a trick?

[*Enter Proteus and Julia.*]

56. **hangman's boys:** boys destined for the gallows.
62. **still an end:** always.
63. **entertained:** employed.

Pro. Sebastian is thy name? I like thee well,
And will employ thee in some service presently.   40
    Jul. In what you please: I'll do what I can.
    Pro. I hope thou wilt. [*To Launce*] How now, you
        whoreson peasant!
Where have you been these two days loitering?
    Launce. Marry, sir, I carried Mistress Silvia the dog   45
you bade me.
    Pro. And what says she to my little jewel?
    Launce. Marry, she says your dog was a cur, and
tells you currish thanks is good enough for such a
present.   50
    Pro. But she received my dog?
    Launce. No, indeed, did she not: here have I
brought him back again.
    Pro. What, didst thou offer her this from me?
    Launce. Ay, sir; the other squirrel was stolen from   55
me by the hangman's boys in the market place; and
then I offered her mine own, who is a dog as big as
ten of yours and therefore the gift the greater.
    Pro. Go, get thee hence and find my dog again,
Or ne'er return again into my sight.   60
Away, I say! Stayest thou to vex me here?
                                        [*Exit Launce.*]
A slave, that still an end turns me to shame!
Sebastian, I have entertained thee,
Partly that I have need of such a youth,
That can with some discretion do my business,   65
For 'tis no trusting to yond foolish lout;
But chiefly for thy face and thy behavior,
Which, if my augury deceive me not,

73. She loved me well: the word "who" should be understood following "well."

74. leave: give up.

Witness good bringing-up, fortune, and truth.
Therefore know thou, for this I entertain thee.   70
Go presently, and take this ring with thee;
Deliver it to Madam Silvia.
She loved me well delivered it to me.

Jul. It seems you loved not her, to leave her token.
She is dead, belike?   75

Pro.   Not so; I think she lives.

Jul. Alas!

Pro. Why dost thou cry "alas"?

Jul.   I cannot choose
But pity her.   80

Pro.   Wherefore shouldst thou pity her?

Jul. Because methinks that she loved you as well
As you do love your lady Silvia:
She dreams on him that has forgot her love;
You dote on her that cares not for your love.   85
'Tis pity love should be so contrary;
And thinking on it makes me cry "alas!"

Pro. Well, give her that ring and therewithal
This letter. That's her chamber. Tell my lady
I claim the promise for her heavenly picture.   90
Your message done, hie home unto my chamber,
Where thou shalt find me, sad and solitary.   [*Exit.*]

Jul. How many women would do such a message?
Alas, poor Proteus! thou hast entertained
A fox to be the shepherd of thy lambs.   95
Alas, poor fool! why do I pity him
That with his very heart despiseth me?
Because he loves her, he despiseth me;
Because I love him, I must pity him.

104. **would have refused:** i.e., would like the receiver to refuse.

125. **unadvised:** thoughtlessly.

This ring I gave him when he parted from me,   100
To bind him to remember my good will;
And now am I, unhappy messenger,
To plead for that which I would not obtain,
To carry that which I would have refused,
To praise his faith which I would have dispraised.   105
I am my master's true-confirmed love,
But cannot be true servant to my master,
Unless I prove false traitor to myself.
Yet will I woo for him, but yet so coldly,
As, Heaven it knows, I would not have him speed.   110

[*Enter Silvia, attended.*]

Gentlewoman, good day! I pray you, be my mean
To bring me where to speak with Madam Silvia.
    Sil. What would you with her, if that I be she?
    Jul. If you be she, I do entreat your patience
To hear me speak the message I am sent on.   115
    Sil. From whom?
    Jul. From my master, Sir Proteus, madam.
    Sil. O, he sends you for a picture?
    Jul. Ay, madam.
    Sil. Ursula, bring my picture there.   120
Go give your master this: tell him, from me,
One Julia, that his changing thoughts forget,
Would better fit his chamber than this shadow.
    Jul. Madam, please you peruse this letter.
Pardon me, madam; I have, unadvised,   125
Delivered you a paper that I should not:
This is the letter to your Ladyship.

143. **tender:** have a care of.
151. **passing:** surpassingly.

Sil. I pray thee, let me look on that again.
Jul. It may not be; good madam, pardon me.
Sil. There, hold!   130
I will not look upon your master's lines:
I know they are stuffed with protestations,
And full of new-found oaths, which he will break
As easily as I do tear his paper.
 Jul. Madam, he sends your Ladyship this ring.   135
 Sil. The more shame for him that he sends it me;
For I have heard him say a thousand times
His Julia gave it him at his departure.
Though his false finger have profaned the ring,
Mine shall not do his Julia so much wrong.   140
 Jul. She thanks you.
 Sil. What sayst thou?
 Jul. I thank you, madam, that you tender her.
Poor gentlewoman! my master wrongs her much.
 Sil. Dost thou know her?   145
 Jul. Almost as well as I do know myself:
To think upon her woes, I do protest
That I have wept a hundred several times.
 Sil. Belike she thinks that Proteus hath forsook her?
 Jul. I think she doth; and that's her cause of sorrow. 150
 Sil. Is she not passing fair?
 Jul. She hath been fairer, madam, than she is:
When she did think my master loved her well,
She, in my judgment, was as fair as you;
But since she did neglect her looking glass,   155
And threw her sun-expelling mask away,
The air hath starved the roses in her cheeks
And pinched the lily-tincture of her face,

159. **black:** swarthy.

164. **trimmed:** decked out.

169. **lamentable:** doleful.

170. **Ariadne:** the daughter of Minos, who helped Theseus kill the Minotaur and escape from the labyrinth, only to be abandoned by him on the island of Naxos.

185. **cold:** poorly received.

186. **my mistress:** i.e., herself.

189. **tire:** headdress.

That now she is become as black as I.
  Sil. How tall was she?   160
  Jul. About my stature: for, at Pentecost,
When all our pageants of delight were played,
Our youth got me to play the woman's part,
And I was trimmed in Madam Julia's gown;
Which served me as fit, by all men's judgments,   165
As if the garment had been made for me:
Therefore I know she is about my height.
And at that time I made her weep agood,
For I did play a lamentable part:
Madam, 'twas Ariadne, passioning   170
For Theseus' perjury and unjust flight;
Which I so lively acted with my tears
That my poor mistress, moved therewithal,
Wept bitterly; and would I might be dead
If I in thought felt not her very sorrow!   175
  Sil. She is beholding to thee, gentle youth.
Alas, poor lady, desolate and left!
I weep myself to think upon thy words.
Here, youth, there is my purse: I give thee this
For thy sweet mistress' sake, because thou lovest her. 180
Farewell.   *Exit Silvia, with attendants.*
  Jul. And she shall thank you for't, if e'er you know
    her.
A virtuous gentlewoman, mild and beautiful!
I hope my master's suit will be but cold,   185
Since she respects my mistress' love so much.
Alas, how love can trifle with itself!
Here is her picture. Let me see: I think,
If I had such a tire, this face of mine

198. **respects:** values.
199. **respective:** worthy of regard.
205. **statue:** idol.

Were full as lovely as is this of hers: 190
And yet the painter flattered her a little,
Unless I flatter with myself too much.
Her hair is auburn, mine is perfect yellow:
If that be all the difference in his love,
I'll get me such a colored periwig.   195
Her eyes are grey as glass, and so are mine:
Ay, but her forehead's low, and mine's as high.
What should it be that he respects in her
But I can make respective in myself,
If this fond Love were not a blinded god?   200
Come, shadow, come, and take this shadow up,
For 'tis thy rival. O thou senseless form,
Thou shalt be worshiped, kissed, loved, and adored!
And, were there sense in his idolatry,
My substance should be statue in thy stead.   205
I'll use thee kindly for thy mistress' sake,
That used me so; or else, by Jove I vow,
I should have scratched out your unseeing eyes,
To make my master out of love with thee!

Exit.

THE
TWO GENTLEMEN
OF
VERONA

ACT V

V.i. Eglamour and Silvia meet and set out for the nearby forest.

▬▬▬▬▬▬▬▬▬▬▬

4. **break not hours:** fail not in keeping appointments.

13. **recover:** reach; **sure:** safe.

ACT V

Scene I. [Milan. An abbey.]

Enter Eglamour.

Egla. The sun begins to gild the western sky,
And now it is about the very hour
That Silvia at Friar Patrick's cell should meet me.
She will not fail, for lovers break not hours,
Unless it be to come before their time;   5
So much they spur their expedition.
See where she comes.

[*Enter Silvia.*]

           Lady, a happy evening!
  Sil. Amen, amen! Go on, good Eglamour,
Out at the postern by the abbey wall: 10
I fear I am attended by some spies.
  Egla. Fear not: the forest is not three leagues off.
If we recover that, we are sure enough.

                        Exeunt.

V.ii. Proteus pretends to encourage Thurio, who realizes that his suit is not progressing. The Duke, seeking Eglamour and Silvia, guesses that they have fled to find Valentine. Proteus, Thurio, the Duke, and Julia all pursue them in the direction of Mantua.

━━━━━━━━━━━━━━━━━━━

14. **pearls:** i.e., cataracts.
16. **wink:** close my eyes.

Scene II. [Milan. The Duke's palace.]

Enter Thurio, Proteus, and Julia.

Thu. Sir Proteus, what says Silvia to my suit?
Pro. O, sir, I find her milder than she was;
And yet she takes exceptions at your person.
Thu. What, that my leg is too long?
Pro. No; that it is too little.   5
Thu. I'll wear a boot, to make it somewhat rounder.
Jul. [*Aside*] But love will not be spurred to what it
    loathes.
Thu. What says she to my face?
Pro. She says it is a fair one.   10
Thu. Nay, then, the wanton lies; my face is black.
Pro. But pearls are fair; and the old saying is,
"Black men are pearls in beauteous ladies' eyes."
Jul. [*Aside*] 'Tis true, such pearls as put out ladies'
    eyes;   15
For I had rather wink than look on them.
Thu. How likes she my discourse?
Pro. Ill, when you talk of war.
Thu. But well, when I discourse of love and peace?
Jul. [*Aside*] But better, indeed, when you hold your   20
    peace.
Thu. What says she to my valor?
Pro. O, sir, she makes no doubt of that.
Jul. [*Aside*] She needs not, when she knows it cow-
    ardice.   25

32. **owe:** possess.
50. **likelihoods:** indications.

Thu. What says she to my birth?

Pro. That you are well derived.

Jul. [*Aside*] True; from a gentleman to a fool.

Thu. Considers she my possessions?

Pro. O, ay; and pities them.   30

Thu. Wherefore?

Jul. [*Aside*] That such an ass should owe them.

Pro. That they are out by lease.

Jul. Here comes the Duke.

[*Enter Duke.*]

Duke. How now, Sir Proteus! How now, Thurio!   35
Which of you saw Sir Eglamour of late?

Thu. Not I.

Pro. Nor I.

Duke.   Saw you my daughter?

Pro.   Neither.   40

Duke. Why then,
She's fled unto that peasant Valentine,
And Eglamour is in her company.
'Tis true; for Friar Laurence met them both,
As he in penance wandered through the forest.   45
Him he knew well, and guessed that it was she,
But, being masked, he was not sure of it.
Besides, she did intend confession
At Patrick's cell this even; and there she was not.
These likelihoods confirm her flight from hence.   50
Therefore, I pray you, stand not to discourse,
But mount you presently and meet with me
Upon the rising of the mountain-foot

56. peevish: foolish.

V.iii. Silvia, captured by the outlaw band, is being taken to their captain—Valentine.

That leads toward Mantua, whither they are fled.
Dispatch, sweet gentlemen, and follow me.   [*Exit.*]   55
    Thu. Why, this it is to be a peevish girl,
That flies her fortune when it follows her.
I'll after, more to be revenged on Eglamour
Than for the love of reckless Silvia.   [*Exit.*]
    Pro. And I will follow, more for Silvia's love   60
Than hate of Eglamour that goes with her.   [*Exit.*]
    Jul. And I will follow, more to cross that love
Than hate for Silvia that is gone for love.

                                    Exit.

Scene III. [The frontiers of Mantua. A forest.]

        [*Enter*] *Outlaws with Silvia.*

    1. Out. Come, come,
Be patient; we must bring you to our captain.
    Sil. A thousand more mischances than this one
Have learned me how to brook this patiently.
    2. Out. Come, bring her away.   5
    1. Out. Where is the gentleman that was with her?
    3. Out. Being nimble-footed, he hath outrun us,
But Moses and Valerius follow him.
Go thou with her to the west end of the wood:
There is our captain. We'll follow him that's fled.   10
The thicket is beset; he cannot 'scape.
    1. Out. Come, I must bring you to our captain's
        cave:
Fear not; he bears an honorable mind

V.iv. Proteus and Julia rescue Silvia from the outlaws but are observed by Valentine as Proteus threatens to force Silvia if she will not give him her love. Valentine reveals himself, disowns his treacherous friend, but relents when Proteus asks forgiveness. Julia swoons when Valentine renounces his claim to Silvia in favor of Proteus. She is recognized and Proteus is overcome with shame and remorse. At this point the outlaws enter with the Duke and Thurio as captives. Valentine orders their release and the Duke relents at this indication of Valentine's nobility. Thurio attempts to press his claim to Silvia but quails when Valentine threatens him. The Duke declares Valentine's recall and his approval of a match between Silvia and Valentine. He further agrees to pardon Valentine's comrades, and all set out for Milan, where the double wedding of the two couples is promised.

▬▬▬▬▬▬▬▬▬▬▬▬▬▬

6. **record:** utter in song (like a bird).

And will not use a woman lawlessly.   15
 Sil. O Valentine, this I endure for thee!

          Exeunt.

Scene IV. [Another part of the forest.]

Enter Valentine.

 Val. How use doth breed a habit in a man!
This shadowy desert, unfrequented woods,
I better brook than flourishing peopled towns:
Here can I sit alone, unseen of any,
And to the nightingale's complaining notes   5
Tune my distresses and record my woes.
O thou that dost inhabit in my breast,
Leave not the mansion so long tenantless,
Lest, growing ruinous, the building fall
And leave no memory of what it was!   10
Repair me with thy presence, Silvia;
Thou gentle nymph, cherish thy forlorn swain!
What halloing and what stir is this today?
These are my mates, that make their wills their law,
Have some unhappy passenger in chase.   15
They love me well; yet I have much to do
To keep them from uncivil outrages.
Withdraw thee, Valentine: who's this comes here?

[*Enter Proteus, Silvia, and Julia.*]

 Pro. Madam, this service I have done for you,
Though you respect not aught your servant doth,   20

45. still approved: ever demonstrated.

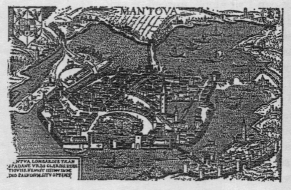

Mantua. From Pietro Bertelli, *Theatrum urbium Italicarum* (1597).

To hazard life and rescue you from him
That would have forced your honor and your love.
Vouchsafe me, for my meed, but one fair look;
A smaller boon than this I cannot beg,
And less than this, I am sure, you cannot give.   25
    Val. [*Aside*] How like a dream is this I see and
        hear!
Love, lend me patience to forbear awhile.
    Sil. O miserable, unhappy that I am!
    Pro. Unhappy were you, madam, ere I came;   30
But by my coming I have made you happy.
    Sil. By thy approach thou makest me most unhappy.
    Jul. [*Aside*] And me, when he approacheth to your
        presence.
    Sil. Had I been seized by a hungry lion,   35
I would have been a breakfast to the beast,
Rather than have false Proteus rescue me.
O, Heaven be judge how I love Valentine,
Whose life's as tender to me as my soul!
And full as much, for more there cannot be,   40
I do detest false perjured Proteus.
Therefore be gone; solicit me no more.
    Pro. What dangerous action, stood it next to death,
Would I not undergo for one calm look!
O, 'tis the curse in love, and still approved,   45
When women cannot love where they're beloved!
    Sil. When Proteus cannot love where he's beloved.
Read over Julia's heart, thy first, best love,
For whose dear sake thou didst then rend thy faith
Into a thousand oaths; and all those oaths   50
Descended into perjury, to love me.

52. **thou'dst:** thou hadst.

68. **common:** ordinary (not special in the way Valentine had thought him to be).

77. **a stranger for thy sake:** i.e., a hostile place because of you.

80. **confounds:** overcomes.

Thou hast no faith left now, unless thou'dst two,
And that's far worse than none; better have none
Than plural faith which is too much by one:
Thou counterfeit to thy true friend!   55
   Pro.   In love
Who respects friend?
   Sil.   All men but Proteus.
   Pro. Nay, if the gentle spirit of moving words
Can no way change you to a milder form,   60
I'll woo you like a soldier, at arm's end,
And love you 'gainst the nature of love—force ye.
   Sil. O Heaven!
   Pro.   I'll force thee yield to my desire.
   Val. Ruffian, let go that rude uncivil touch,   65
Thou friend of an ill fashion!
   Pro.   Valentine!
   Val. Thou common friend, that's without faith or
       love,
For such is a friend now! Treacherous man,   70
Thou hast beguiled my hopes; nought but mine eye
Could have persuaded me. Now I dare not say
I have one friend alive; thou wouldst disprove me.
Who should be trusted now, when one's right hand
Is perjured to the bosom? Proteus,   75
I am sorry I must never trust thee more,
But count the world a stranger for thy sake.
The private wound is deepest. O time most accurst,
'Mongst all foes that a friend should be the worst!
   Pro. My shame and guilt confounds me.   80
Forgive me, Valentine: if hearty sorrow
Be a sufficient ransom for offense,

84. **commit:** i.e., commit offenses.
86. **honest:** honorable.
103. **cry you mercy:** I beg your pardon.
110. **gave aim to:** was the object of.

I tender 't here; I do as truly suffer
As e'er I did commit.

Val.   Then I am paid;   85
And once again I do receive thee honest.
Who by repentance is not satisfied
Is nor of Heaven nor earth, for these are pleased.
By penitence the Eternal's wrath's appeased:
And, that my love may appear plain and free,   90
All that was mine in Silvia I give thee.

Jul. O me unhappy!   [*Swoons.*]

Pro. Look to the boy.

Val. Why, boy! why, wag! how now! what's the
matter? Look up; speak.   95

Jul. O good sir, my master charged me to deliver a
ring to Madam Silvia, which, out of my neglect, was
never done.

Pro. Where is that ring, boy?

Jul.   Here, 'tis; this is it.   100

Pro. How! let me see:
Why, this is the ring I gave to Julia.

Jul. O, cry you mercy, sir, I have mistook:
This is the ring you sent to Silvia.

                         [*Offering another ring.*]

Pro. But how camest thou by this ring? At my de-   105
part I gave this unto Julia.

Jul. And Julia herself did give it me;
And Julia herself hath brought it hither.

Pro. How! Julia!

Jul. Behold her that gave aim to all thy oaths,   110
And entertained 'em deeply in her heart.
How oft hast thou with perjury cleft the root!

113. **this habit:** the apparel she wears.

124. **Inconstancy falls off ere it begins:** i.e., the inconstant man breaks his faith even before he has begun to demonstrate it.

139. **measure:** range (of his sword).

O Proteus, let this habit make thee blush!
Be thou ashamed that I have took upon me
Such an immodest raiment, if shame live   115
In a disguise of love:
It is the lesser blot, modesty finds,
Women to change their shapes than men their minds.
   Pro. Than men their minds! 'tis true. O Heaven,
     were man   120
But constant, he were perfect! That one error
Fills him with faults; makes him run through all the
     sins:
Inconstancy falls off ere it begins.
What is in Silvia's face but I may spy   125
More fresh in Julia's with a constant eye?
   Val. Come, come, a hand from either:
Let me be blest to make this happy close;
'Twere pity two such friends should be long foes.
   Pro. Bear witness, Heaven, I have my wish forever. 130
   Jul. And I mine.

        [Enter Outlaws, with Duke and Thurio.]

   Outlaws. A prize, a prize, a prize!
   Val. Forbear, forbear, I say! it is my lord the Duke.
Your Grace is welcome to a man disgraced,
Banished Valentine.   135
   Duke.   Sir Valentine!
   Thu. Yonder is Silvia; and Silvia's mine.
   Val. Thurio, give back, or else embrace thy death!
Come not within the measure of my wrath.
Do not name Silvia thine. If once again,   140

149. **means:** efforts.

154. **griefs:** grievances.

156. **Plead a new state in thy unrivaled merit:** plead in defense of my action that your unrivaled merit alters your worldly status.

166. **endued:** endowed.

Verona shall not hold thee. Here she stands:
Take but possession of her with a touch!
I dare thee but to breathe upon my love.
   Thu. Sir Valentine, I care not for her, I:
I hold him but a fool that will endanger   145
His body for a girl that loves him not.
I claim her not, and therefore she is thine.
   Duke. The more degenerate and base art thou,
To make such means for her as thou hast done
And leave her on such slight conditions.   150
Now, by the honor of my ancestry,
I do applaud thy spirit, Valentine,
And think thee worthy of an empress' love:
Know, then, I here forget all former griefs,
Cancel all grudge, repeal thee home again,   155
Plead a new state in thy unrivaled merit,
To which I thus subscribe: Sir Valentine,
Thou art a gentleman and well derived.
Take thou thy Silvia, for thou hast deserved her.
   Val. I thank your Grace; the gift hath made me 160
     happy.
I now beseech you, for your daughter's sake,
To grant one boon that I shall ask of you.
   Duke. I grant it, for thine own, whate'er it be.
   Val. These banished men that I have kept withal 165
Are men endued with worthy qualities:
Forgive them what they have committed here
And let them be recalled from their exile.
They are reformed, civil, full of good,
And fit for great employment, worthy lord.   170

174. **include:** conclude; **jars:** dissensions.
175. **triumphs:** pageants; **solemnity:** festivity.

Duke. Thou hast prevailed; I pardon them and
   thee:
Dispose of them as thou knowst their deserts.
Come, let us go; we will include all jars
With triumphs, mirth, and rare solemnity.   175

Val. And, as we walk along, I dare be bold
With our discourse to make your Grace to smile.
What think you of this page, my lord?
   Duke. I think the boy hath grace in him: he blushes.
   Val. I warrant you, my lord, more grace than boy.   180
   Duke. What mean you by that saying?
   Val. Please you, I'll tell you as we pass along,
That you will wonder what hath fortuned.
Come, Proteus, 'tis your penance but to hear
The story of your loves discovered.   185
That done, our day of marriage shall be yours:
One feast, one house, one mutual happiness.

                                        Exeunt.

KEY TO
Famous Lines

Homekeeping youth have ever homely wits.

[*Valentine*—I.i.2]

I have no other but a woman's reason:
I think him so because I think him so.

[*Lucetta*—I.ii.25–26]

They do not love that do not show their
love.

[*Julia*—I.ii.34]

The uncertain glory of an April day.

[*Proteus*—I.iii.89]

What light is light, if Silvia be not seen?
What joy is joy, if Silvia be not by?
Unless it be to think that she is by,
And feed upon the shadow of perfection.

[*Valentine*—III.i.179–82]

Love/Will creep in service where it
cannot go.

[*Proteus*—IV.ii.19–20]

Who is Silvia? what is she . . .

[*Song*—IV.ii.39–53]

How use doth breed a habit in a man!

[*Valentine*—V.iv.1]